CHARMING

A BIG SKY NOVEL

Hannah

NEW YORK TIMES BEST SELLING AUTHOR

KRISTEN PROBY

CHARMING HANNAH
A Big Sky Novel
Kristen Proby

Photography by: Sara Eirew Photographer
Cover and Formatting Design: Uplifting Designs

ISBN: 978-1-63350-031-0

Other Books by Kristen Proby

The Big Sky Series
Charming Hannah
Kissing Jenna – Coming soon
Waiting for Willa – Coming soon

The Fusion Series
Listen To Me
Close To You
Blush For Me
The Beauty of Us
Savor You – Coming soon

The Boudreaux Series
Easy Love
Easy Charm
Easy Melody
Easy Kisses
Easy Magic
Easy Fortune
Easy Nights

The With Me In Seattle Series
Come Away With Me
Under the Mistletoe With Me
Fight With Me
Play With Me
Rock With Me
Safe With Me

Tied With Me
Breathe With Me
Forever With Me

The Love Under the Big Sky Series
Loving Cara
Seducing Lauren
Falling For Jillian
Saving Grace

From 1001 Dark Nights
Easy With You
Easy For Keeps
No Reservations
Tempting Brooke – Coming soon

The Romancing Manhattan Series
All the Way – Coming soon

CHARMING

A BIG SKY NOVEL

Hannah

PROLOGUE

Brad

Three years ago...

"WOULD YOU LIKE ANOTHER glass of champagne?" I ask Hannah, the tall red headed doctor standing next to me. We're at an exclusive party on Whitetail Mountain, with the owner of the ski resort and all of my closest friends.

"One is enough for me," she says with a smile, showing off her dimples. I can't help but wonder if she has dimples above her ass as well. I've seen her around town since she moved here, taking a position as a doctor, and each time I see her the lust is swift and hard.

She's sexy as fuck.

And I want her.

But I'm also a gentleman. Seeing her here was an unexpected treat.

I pass her a bottle of water and then walk with her out onto the deck where a fire is going to keep us all warm. The torch light parade is over, and people are beginning to leave. But I stand here with Hannah, leaning on the railing and watching people bustle between the two bars in the ski village.

"It's beautiful up here," she murmurs.

I nod and sip my bottle of water. "Do you like Cunningham Falls?"

"It's paradise," she murmurs and then smiles up at me. "I know it sounds corny, but that's what I think of it. The mountains, the small town, the people. I couldn't love it more."

I feel the same way.

But I've lived here all my life, so maybe I'm biased.

"How long have you been a cop?" she asks.

"Almost fifteen years. My dad is the police chief." I shrug. "I never wanted to be anything else."

"Do you think you'll be the police chief after he leaves?"

I shrug again. My application is already in for it, but who knows if I'll get hired?

"We'll see." I hook her red hair behind her ear. My sister Jenna walks over to us, her coat wrapped around her shoulders.

"I'm ready to head out, Hannah. How about you?"

Hannah glances up at me. "I rode with Jenna. Looks like we're ready to go."

"I can give you a ride," I offer and Jenna's eyes widen with surprise.

"Oh, you don't have—" Hannah begins but Jenna cuts her off.

"That's a great idea. I have some work to do this evening anyway, so if Brad can give you a lift, that's perfect. I'll talk to you later!" And with that, she waves and leaves Hannah with a stunned smile on her beautiful face.

"Looks like you're stuck with me."

"Are you sure you don't mind?"

I shake my head and lead her inside to gather our coats and say our goodbyes to Jacob and Grace, the hosts of the party. Once in my truck, Hannah gets comfortable in the leather passenger seat and sighs.

"Are you okay?"

"I'm tired," she confesses. "I was at the hospital all last night, but I didn't want to miss this party. I'm glad I came."

"I am too."

I concentrate on the slippery road that winds down the mountain to town. Once we're on the main, better travelled street, I feel more comfortable. It's been snowing heavily, and the mountain road is always tricky. But about a mile later, we come upon an accident.

"Two cars," I mutter and slow to a stop. I immediately reach for my phone to call it in, and Hannah has leapt from the truck, moving quickly toward the car with the most damage.

Thank God it's no one from the party.

"Over here," Hannah calls after I shove my phone in my pocket. She's standing by the driver's side of a small sedan, the door open, and the young woman driver is passed out against the steering wheel. "She's unconscious, but she's alive. I don't want to move her until the paramedics get here. I don't know what her injuries are. Will you stay with her while I check the other car?"

"No need," someone says from behind us. "I'm fine. My God, I couldn't stop the car when I went into a full spin."

"It's okay," Hannah says, turning around and immediately taking her scarf off and pressing it to a bloody gash on the man's forehead. "Hold this to your head. You have a small laceration there."

"I do?"

"He's in shock," she says to me, just as we hear the sirens coming in the distance. "Paramedics are on the way," she says to him and urges him to sit on the snow bank, holding the scarf to his head.

The young woman is coming to, and when she looks around, she starts to cry.

"It's okay," I say and rub my hand up and down

her arm soothingly. "You've been in an accident, but help is on the way."

The next ten minutes are a blur as the ambulance arrives. Hannah rattles off a quick report of what happened and the paramedics load both of the injured drivers inside, then heads to the hospital. I stay an extra five minutes to help the officers on scene, and when Hannah and I are back in my truck, she says, "Take me to the hospital."

She doesn't look tired now, and watching her on the scene was amazing.

"Are you sure?"

"I want to check on them before I go home," she says. "I know I'm an OB/GYN, but they're mine now."

I nod and pull into the emergency bay behind the ambulance. Hannah jumps out and I see her give a quick report to a doctor that walks up – one she appears to know – and it's amazing to see her in her own element.

I've never been more turned on in my life.

She's stunning, her blue eyes bright and red hair around her face. She's a force to be reckoned with.

After all of her reports are given to the doctors on staff, she blows out a breath and returns to me with a shy smile. "Sorry, I just needed to see this through."

"No need to be sorry." I can't keep myself from dragging my finger down her cheek. "Are you okay?"

"Of course."

"Hannah!"

Both of us turn at the sound of her name. A tall doctor, Drake I believe his name is, rushes to her and cups her face in his hands.

"Are you okay?"

"I'm fine. I wasn't in the accident."

"Thank God." He pulls her in for a hug, and it's clear that they're close. Intimate.

Together.

So while they're hugging and she's telling him all about what happened, I slip out the door to my truck.

The sexy doctor isn't available.

Fuck.

CHAPTER ONE

Hannah

"I'M GOING TO DIE."

"I'm one hundred percent sure that you're not going to die today," my best friend, Drake, says with a smirk.

A freaking *smirk.*

"How do you know?"

"I'm a doctor," he says and reaches over to steal a donut hole from my plate. "I went to school for a really long time so I could tell hypochondriacs like you that you aren't dying."

I narrow my eyes and watch him, sitting all smug like across from me. We're at our favorite café in town, Drips & Sips, sitting outside for the first time this summer, now that the weather is finally nice enough to allow it.

It's a breezy seventy degrees, yet there is still some snow clinging to life at the top of the ski mountain that's directly in my view.

It doesn't suck to live here.

"You can't tell just by looking at me that I'm not dying."

"Okay," he says and takes a big bite of his scone. "Why do you think you're dying?"

"My low back has been *killing* me," I reply. "I have twinges in the ovary area. I'm pretty sure I must have ovarian cancer."

"Or, you have a back ache and you're ovulating," he replies, and I want to slap him for being so flippant about it all.

"Drake—"

"Hannah Banana, I love you, more than you'll ever know. But I'm going to say this to you, again, and it probably won't be the last time. You're an amazing doctor, but you never should have gone to medical school. You know too much. A twinge here and there isn't cancer."

I try to speak, but he holds a finger up and keeps talking.

"It *isn't*. You're a healthy thirty-five year old woman with a great career, ridiculously attractive friends, and you make enough money to buy yourself a pretty condo pretty much anywhere in the world. Stop buying trouble with the whole dying thing."

"You're not *that* attractive," I reply and fidget with the silverware on the tabletop, trying not to sulk.

"Yes, I am," he says and flashes his annoyingly perfect teeth at me.

"I have been on my feet a lot lately," I concede and pop a donut hole in my mouth. "Lots of babies decided to show up this week."

"There you go," he says. "Not cancer."

I sigh and nod, feeling stupid. "Why do I do this to myself?"

"Because you've seen first hand what illness can do. It's scary."

"Also, being a doctor means that we're confronted with our mortality all the time."

"True."

"I don't think this is unusual."

"It's not."

"So I'm not crazy."

"I didn't say that," he replies with a grin, and I finally laugh.

"You're supposed to be my best friend and make me feel better." I kick out with my foot, connecting with his shin.

"Ouch." He laughs and rubs his shin. "You're a violent woman, Hannah."

"Yeah, well, you can take it."

Suddenly Drake's phone begins to ring.

"It's the hospital," he says grimly. "This is Dr. Merritt."

He listens quietly for a moment, then tosses his napkin on the table and I know our breakfast is over.

"I'll be there in ten." He ends the call. "Gotta run. Appendectomy."

"Good luck." He reaches for his wallet, but I shake my head. "Go. I've got this. You get it next time."

"Thanks." He smiles but his head is already in the surgery. He jogs over to his brand new Land Rover and speeds away, leaving me here in downtown Cunningham Falls to enjoy the morning sunshine and to eavesdrop on the couple who just sat down at the table next to ours.

It's not going well.

"I can't believe you're doing this in public," the brunette woman says with tears in her voice.

"At least it wasn't by text," the man replies, and I frown, then hide my face behind my almost empty coffee mug. What a jerk.

"So, why now? I thought it was going well."

There's a long pause, and then the douchebag replies with, "I'm going to be brutally honest here. The sex just isn't doing it for me."

"We haven't even *had* sex yet," she hisses, and he has the audacity to simply nod.

"Exactly."

"You said you understood when I told you that I wanted to get to know you better first."

"Yeah, I thought you meant that you had a stupid three date rule or something. But it's been a month, Penny, and *nada*."

"I'm relieved I didn't have sex with you, and I regret the blow job."

"That was a delightful evening," he says with a wink, and I silently will the woman to punch him in the throat.

But she does something *so much better.*

She stands, and says in the loudest voice possible without shouting, "No, Nick, your limp dick issue isn't normal. You should see someone about that. Not to mention, you couldn't find a woman's g-spot with GPS *and* written instructions. You should probably see someone about that, too. Your inability to please a woman is embarrassing, and I need a *real* man in my life."

With that, she turns and stomps away, chin up, not a tear in sight. And I can't help but stand and give her a slow clap, then turn and glare at Mr. Douchenozzle. He's not smirking now, is he?

He curses and rushes away in the opposite direction, and I sit back with what's left of my coffee, ready to enjoy the last few moments before I have to go to the office.

I tip my face back to soak in some sunshine and revel in the mountain views. The fact that the snow is still holding on at the top is surprising for this late in the year.

It was a particularly snowy winter, and by the

time it started to melt, I'd seriously questioned whether I made the right choice in accepting the position here five years ago. I'd originally wanted to settle in a city, delivering a dozen babies a day. I *love* my job, and after putting in my time at big city offices, I didn't know if that was for me, either. I want to develop a working relationship with my patients, not just shuffle them through the office, one after the other, as fast as I can.

When Drake told me there was a position open here, I brushed it off, still not convinced that this was for me. I'd been here to visit, and while it's beautiful, I didn't think small town life was the answer.

I'd left that behind when I was eighteen and finally able to escape the home life from hell for college. A *full ride* scholarship, for the first four years, followed by a mountain of loans that I've thankfully been able to pay down quickly. I don't owe anyone anything, and I earned everything that I now have.

But Cunningham Falls, Montana, is nothing like Wamego, Kansas. There are mountains here. Fewer bugs. More people. And that's saying a lot, given that Cunningham Falls has fewer than ten thousand full time residents.

This is also the biggest and bluest sky I've ever seen, when it isn't winter anyway.

And most importantly, there is no Randall Malone here. No, I ran far from that man and his liquor.

His self destruction.

No child should bear the burden of an alcoholic father. I don't know if he's dead yet. Part of me hopes so. I could do a search. With social media and Google being what it is, it probably wouldn't be hard to find out.

But I haven't looked because honestly, it doesn't matter. He's not even a spot in the rear-view mirror anymore.

"Hello, Hannah."

I turn and shield my eyes from the sun, delighted to see Lauren Cunningham. Actually, Lauren Sullivan now that she's married to Ty.

She rests her hand on her gently rounded belly and grins.

"Hi, Lauren. Wanna have a seat?"

"Are you alone?" she asks and sits in the chair that Drake just vacated.

"Drake had to run off to a surgery. I thought I'd enjoy the sunshine for a minute."

"It's beautiful today," she says with a grin. "It's about time summer showed up."

"How are you feeling?"

"Great." She pats her belly again. "I had no idea that pregnancies could be so different. This isn't anything at all like my first."

"They say no two babies come into this world in the same way, and from what I hear, that's the truth."

She nods and tips her head back so the sun beats on her face. "I'm on my way to see Ty. I thought I'd take him an early lunch."

"That's romantic."

She grins. "And a great excuse to procrastinate. I'm supposed to be writing."

"It'll still be there later."

"And my editor will be happy to remind me."

Her name is called inside, and she stands. "That's me. Enjoy your sunshine, Hannah. I'll see you next week."

"Have a great day."

She leaves, and I check my phone for the time. I need to get to the office. My appointments for the day started late, which I like because sleeping in is my jam. Most babies think it's hilarious to make their grand entrance in the middle of the night, so I take as many mornings as I can off. I also agreed to go to a party this evening for some leggings that are supposed to be the most comfortable thing in the world.

I have no idea why I have to go to a party to buy them, like Tupperware, instead of just buying them in a store, but nevertheless, I agreed to go.

I'm regretting that now.

If it makes me a bad person to secretly hope and pray that someone, *anyone,* goes into labor so I don't have to go to that party, well, then I guess I'm a bad person.

I toss my trash in the garbage and get in my car, already thinking about my first appointment. I back out of my parking space, and *bam!*

I'm rear-ended.

I lay my forehead on the steering wheel. I don't have time for this. I wasted all of my extra time drinking coffee with Drake and basking in the sunshine. I whip my seatbelt off and jump out of my car, ready to survey the damage.

And stepping out of his red truck is Brad Hull.

Tall, broad, soft-spoken Brad Hull, who also happens to be a cop in Cunningham Falls.

Not just *any* cop. No, he's the newly appointed chief of police.

And sexier than just about any man I've ever seen.

And trust me when I say, I've seen a lot of men. Not necessarily intimately, but I've seen them just the same.

"Are you okay?" he asks.

"I'm fine. You must not have been going very fast."

His lips twitch, making me wonder what's so funny.

"I was stopped dead," he replies. "You ran into me."

"Uh, no, I didn't." I prop my hands on my hips and do my best to glare at him. It helps that the sunshine is so bright.

"You did."

I frown and look at our vehicles, relieved to see that there's no damage.

"I definitely didn't run into you. I looked in my mirror and no one was there."

He nods twice. "Or, I was there, but you were thinking of other things."

"Are you calling me a liar?"

"No, ma'am," he says immediately. "I'm not on duty, and there's no damage. But I am not lying either when I say that I was not moving when you hit me."

I narrow my eyes and take a long, deep breath. "Are you going to handcuff me?"

His eyebrows climb in surprise, and I can't help but laugh.

"I don't mean like that."

"Well, that's too bad."

I laugh again and brush my hair over my shoulder. "Am I in trouble?"

"No."

"I'm not going to be arrested?"

"No, ma'am."

I nod. "Great. I have to get to work."

"We should exchange numbers," he says with a smile. "That's the customary thing to do when you're in an accident."

"We weren't—" I shake my head. "Fine." I reach in my car and grab a card out of my purse. "Here's my number. Let me know if I need to cover any damage done to your truck."

"Will do," he says. "Drive safely."

I wrinkle my nose at him and climb back in the car, late for my first appointment. Starting the day already behind doesn't bode well. Just as I pull in the parking lot of my practice, my phone pings with a text.

We should have dinner tonight to discuss our accident.

I laugh out loud as I reply.

I already have plans tonight.

As I reach for the door, it pings again.

Tomorrow night, then. You can't say no. I'm the law.

I bite my lip, thinking it over, and decide what the hell.

Fine, but you're buying me dinner.

Deal.

Not one baby in this whole town decided to save me from the leggings party this evening. Which means that rather than go home and change into something comfy so I can binge watch a whole season of Scandal on Netflix, I'm sitting in my dear friend Grace's living room, watching other women I don't know browse through racks and racks of not just leggings, but also tops, dresses, and kimonos as well.

I'm standing in the corner with a Coke in my hand, chatting with Grace.

"This house still makes my jaw drop," I inform her as I stare up at her cathedral ceiling. Grace and her new husband, Jacob, live in a multi-million dollar home on the lake, complete with boathouse and slip. Jacob is a real estate mogul from England who happened to purchase the ski resort, along with several local restaurants, in the past few years. But the most important thing is, no matter how much money Jacob has, he makes my friend ridiculously happy.

"It's pretty," she says with a nod. "I told Jacob that I didn't need anything this fancy, but he says it's an investment, and he likes to give me nice things."

"Well, no one can fault him for that." I clink my glass to hers and then stare at all of the clothes in this room. "Have you worn any of this before?"

"I have lots of leggings," she says with a nod. "They're super soft and I like to wear them around the house. But I haven't worn any of the other things. I just wanted to give Penny a chance to grow her business a bit."

"Penny?" I scan the room, and sure enough, there she is. The woman who got dumped and then castrated the moron with words. "Is that her?"

"It is. Do you know her?"

I shake my head and tell her about this morning outside of Drips & Sips.

"Oh, that sucks," Grace says with a grimace. "She really liked him."

"How do you know her?"

"She's a teacher at the school."

I nod. Grace teaches at the local middle school.

"Well, she handled herself very well."

"Sounds like her. She's smart."

Grace gets pulled away to mingle with the other women. I recognize Cara King and her best friend Jillian King, who married brothers about three years ago. I've met them before, but I wouldn't say we're close friends.

In fact, aside from Grace, Drake, and my cousin Abby, I wouldn't say I'm close friends with *anyone*.

And I'm not sure if that's entirely normal or healthy.

"Why are you all by yourself over here?" Jenna Hull, Brad's younger sister, asks. She's smiling as she passes me another Coke.

"I'm really an observer," I reply with a grateful smile. "Thanks for the refill."

"No wine for you?" she asks as Grace joins us again.

"I don't drink. I'm pretty much always on call, unless I'm on vacation, so it's best if I stay sober."

"Wow," Jenna says with a frown. Even with the frown, she's probably the most beautiful woman I've ever seen. With light blonde hair and bright blue eyes, she's a dead ringer for Kristen Bell. "I guess it never occurred to me that you're on call 24/7."

"There are only four obstetricians in town," I remind her. "And I know that my patients prefer to have me deliver their babies if at all possible, so I make myself available to them."

"I'm sure they appreciate that," Grace says with a nod. "But you should take some time for yourself, too. I've been nagging you about this for years."

"I do," I lie.

"She just lied to you," Grace informs Jenna, who nods in agreement.

"I *do*," I insist.

"Really?" Jenna asks. "What was the last thing you did just for you?"

"I agreed to have dinner with your brother to-morrow night," I reply before I can stop myself, and take a gulp of my soda.

Damn it.

"Seriously?" Grace asks and does a little ex-cited jig, then almost falls over. I love Grace like a sister, and one of the things I love most about her is her clumsiness.

"You don't say," Jenna says with a grin. "Good

for you. Brad's a nice guy, and I'm not just saying that because I'm biased."

"You're totally biased," I reply with a laugh.

"True, but aside from the sister bias, I still think he's a great person."

"And, he's hot," Grace says with a nod.

"I wouldn't say *hot*," Jenna says, wrinkling her nose.

"That's because he's your brother," I reply with a laugh. "And I have to side with Grace. He's a handsome fella."

"Where are you going for dinner?" Grace asks.

"I have no idea. We didn't get that far. I'm assuming he'll just pick me up and take me somewhere."

"How fun," Grace says. "A first date with someone new. It's so romantic."

"Yeah, unless I choke on something or say the wrong thing." I shrug. "It could be a nightmare. But he's nice. And he offered to buy me dinner, and let's face it, a girl shouldn't pass that up."

"Absolutely not," Grace says. "Free dinner with a handsome date, who just happens to be the new chief of police? That doesn't suck at all."

"You'll have fun," Jenna agrees. "Despite being a cop, my brother is pretty laid back. There's no pressure."

"Well, that's good because I haven't been on a date in—" I check my watch "about a year and a half."

"That's a long time," Jenna says with wide eyes. "Don't you miss having sex?"

"Who has time?" I ask with a laugh.

"Trust me, when it comes to sex, you *make* time," Grace replies and pats my shoulder as if in sympathy. "And as hot as Brad is, the sex is going to be off the charts."

"Ew," Jenna says, wrinkling her nose again. "Don't ever say those words again."

"He's your brother, not a eunuch," Grace reminds her.

"I'm not having sex with him on the first date." *Probably*.

"Good," Jenna says. "Make him work for it. Too many women throw themselves at him because he *is* a cop and, rumor has it, hot."

"Super hot," Grace adds with a nod.

"I'm not throwing myself at him. Why would anyone do that?"

"Exactly," Jenna agrees. "I mean, women need to have more self respect. Like any guy who has his shit together is going to want to be with someone who throws themselves at them."

"Guys like a chase," Grace adds. "It's good that you're not going to be slutty."

I can't help but cover my mouth and giggle. "I can't believe we're having this conversation."

"I'm *ecstatic* that we're having this conversation," Grace says. "You deserve to do something just for you, and going on a date is a huge step for you."

"Are you a virgin?" Jenna asks, and if I'm not mistaken, there's a thread of mortification in her voice.

"No." I laugh again. "Definitely not a virgin. I just don't have time to date. People around here keep having babies."

"I get it," Jenna says. "I don't date much either."

"Are you still running the bed and breakfast on the mountain?" I ask, relieved that the conversation has diverted from me.

"I still own it, but I hired a manager to run it for me. I purchased a few other vacation rentals last year that I take care of, and I have a new secret project."

"Spill it," Grace says.

"Well, keep this between us. Brad, Max, and I have bought some property up near the ski resort, and we're building tree houses to use as vacation rentals."

"Will renters have to bring sleeping bags and know the password to get in?" Grace asks.

"No, not that kind of tree house," Jenna says with a smile. "High end, super fancy tree houses. There will be three of them, and I'm hoping to start renting them out this winter."

"Well, I can't wait to see this," I say.

"We will host a viewing party when they're done and invite our friends to come see them before we open them up for rentals."

"*So* cool," Grace says. "Jacob mentioned to me that he sold a large lot just off of one of the ski runs."

"That's us," Jenna says. "I can't wait to show them off."

Thankfully, the subject turns to work and we trade stories. Grace has hilarious student stories, Jenna has all kinds of tales about horrible renters, and I always have fun tidbits from the babies I've delivered.

It's fun to spend time with friends and laugh. I don't remember the last time I did this.

And, of course, my phone rings with a call from the hospital.

"Looks like someone is having a baby tonight after all."

"Do you have to go?" Jenna asks.

"I do. But thanks for hanging out with me tonight. It was fun."

"Here's my number," Jenna says and presses her business card in my hand. "Text me and fill me in on your date with my darling brother."

"Make it a group text," Grace says with a sassy smile. "I want to hear all about it, too."

"If more babies decide to come, I might have

to cancel."

"Don't cancel," Grace says. "I will punch you in the throat if you do. You *need* this."

"You're quite violent," I reply and reach for my handbag. "Stop threatening to assault me."

"Stop threatening to cancel your date with Chief Sexypants."

"I'm *so* going to start calling him that," Jenna says with a laugh.

"I won't cancel," I say, laughing with them. "I mean, who doesn't want a date with Chief Sexypants?"

"Exactly," Grace says.

CHAPTER TWO

Hannah

I MADE IT OUT of the office on time, and so far, none of my patients are in labor.

It looks like the Fates have decided that this date is a for sure thing, and I'm actually really excited about it. Brad and I have known each other for a while, and I'd be lying if I didn't admit that I'm attracted to him. Chief Sexypants is an accurate name for him. He's tall and broad, with wide shoulders and kind green eyes.

And a really, *really* great ass.

I can't believe I'm finally going out with him. All day today I felt like I was having heart palpitations and giant eagles in my stomach from the nerves. It's not that I'm shy, I'm just out of practice.

And I wasn't terribly good at dating before either. Add that to being out of practice, and only bad things can result from this.

I'm standing in the middle of my bedroom, naked, looking around blindly because I don't know what to do next.

I pick up my phone and call my cousin, Abby.

"Are you ready for your date?" she asks when she answers.

"I'm naked."

"I didn't think you were a first date sex kind of girl, but whatever floats your boat, sweetie."

"Funny." I roll my eyes. "I don't know what to wear. Abby, I only have clothes that I wear to work. And I haven't done laundry in about three weeks, so all of my good underwear are dirty. I *can't* wear period underwear on a first date."

"No. You can't. So go commando."

"That's seriously not sanitary," I reply and frown at the phone.

"Why? You're wearing clean pants."

"I'm an underwear person," I reply. "And all of mine that are clean are ones I wear when it's shark week."

"Well, you're not planning on letting him see your underwear anyway, right?"

"True. And if by some miracle our clothes *do* come off, I'll just have to make sure it's in the dark so he can't see my panties."

"I don't think he'll really care about your panties if you're letting him get inside of them," she says reasonably. I step into my panties and then frown at my feet.

"I haven't had a pedicure."

"Does he have a foot fetish? Jesus, Han, he sounds really pervy."

"This is the first date," I remind her. "I don't know if he has a foot fetish. But my toes are *not* polished."

"Are you wearing flip flops?"

"No, it's still chilly in the evening here. I think I'll wear flats."

"Awesome. We've solved the pedicure debacle. What are you wearing?"

"He didn't say if it was fancy or not."

"Do you have a pretty sun dress that can be either fancy or casual?"

"I have *work clothes,* Abby."

"I gave you a red summer dress last year when I was there."

"Your ass is smaller than mine," I remind her, but shuffle through my closet, looking for the dress. "I found it."

"Try it on."

I pull it over my head and turn to look in the mirror. "Not bad. This will work. I'll take a denim jacket, and that will dress it down a bit if need be."

"Excellent," Abby says. I can hear the smile in her voice. "Makeup?"

"I'm still wearing makeup from work."

"Which means you applied it twelve hours ago.

You need to freshen it up."

"I didn't have time to take a shower," I inform her. "I hope there's no blood in my hair."

"Oh God. Ew. And you're worried about your period panties? Honey, your priorities might be a little skewed."

I chuckle and freshen up my eye makeup, then run a brush through my red hair and shrug one shoulder. "No blood."

"Thank goodness. I'm sure you look great, and you'll have so much fun, Hannah."

"I think so," I murmur. "Unless I choke or get food poisoning or something. Also, I've been having these palpitations today. Maybe I should make an appointment with the cardiologist."

"It's called nerves," she says. "You're not having a heart attack, Hannah, you're nervous about a first date with a cool guy. It's normal."

"But you're not a cardiologist. You don't know."

She takes a deep breath, and I picture her closing her eyes, trying to keep her irritation in check.

"I know," I say at last. "I always do this, and I'm stupid."

"You're not stupid. Take a deep breath."

I breathe in deeply through my nose and let it out through my mouth and feel a little better.

"When will he be there?"

I check the time on my phone.

"Ten minutes."

"Okay, here's what I want you to do. Take some more deep breaths, drink some water, and look at your schedule for tomorrow."

I frown, thrown by that last one. "Why?"

"Because you'll be thinking about tomorrow and not worrying about tonight."

"You're pretty smart."

She snorts. "I know. Have fun and text me when you get home because I'll want to hear how it went."

"Okay." I nod, even though she can't see me. "You're right, I'm just going to enjoy myself and *not* wish that I was at home watching Stranger Things."

"Oh my gosh, have you started season two yet?"

"No, I'm only halfway into season one because instead of watching it I'm going on a date tonight."

"Well, just wait until you get to season two. So good."

"Season one is kind of freaking me out," I admit. "I don't like the scary things."

"It's not that scary. Stick with it. You won't regret it. And look at that, you only have seven minutes now."

"Okay, I'm ready. I'm going to go look at tomorrow's schedule."

"Awesome. Have fun, Han. I mean it."

"I will. Talk to you later."

I hang up the phone and blow out a breath. There's no need to be nervous. He's just a man. A human.

I mean, sure, this human is better looking than most others, and the chemistry I feel when I'm in the same room as him is like nothing I've ever felt before.

But he's still just a man.

I throw the load of laundry I put in the washer this morning into the dryer, flip it on, then walk into the kitchen to rinse a few dishes and put them in the dishwasher.

I bring my schedule for tomorrow up on my phone just as the doorbell rings.

"Those were a quick seven minutes," I mutter. I run my fingers through my hair before opening the door to Brad.

He's leaning on the doorjamb, a crooked smile on his mouth and his green eyes are happy. I let myself take him in from head to toe, admiring the grey sweater and dark blue jeans, and the way they showcase his hard, lean body.

"Hi," I say and step back so he can come inside, ignoring the knowing smile on his lips.

"Hello, beautiful," he replies and passes me a bouquet of pink roses. "These are for you."

"Oh, how nice." I bury my nose in them and smile up at him. "Thank you. I'll put them in water real quick before we go."

He nods and follows me into the kitchen. "Your home is nice."

"Thanks." I wrinkle my nose at him. "I'm not here much, so it doesn't get very dirty. I don't know why I told you that." I fill a vase with cold water and quickly clip the ends of the blooms before fussing over them.

"Because it's the truth," he says and brushes my hair over my shoulder. "How are you today?"

"Nervous," I admit. "That's the truth, too."

"No need to be nervous, Hannah. It's just dinner."

I nod and take a deep breath, then smile up at him. "Okay. I'm ready."

He laughs and takes my hand, then surprises me by raising it to his lips and gently kissing my knuckles. "It's going to be fun."

"I know."

He watches me for a moment, then, still holding my hand, leads me through the house to the front door. My arm is on fire from the electricity running through it. Jesus, if just the touch of his hand causes this kind of reaction, I can only imagine what would happen if we were naked.

Not that we will be naked tonight.

I grab my jacket and handbag, lock up behind

us, and follow him to his truck.

Once we're settled and headed down the street, he smiles over at me. "I thought we'd head over to *Ciao* for some Italian, if that works for you."

"That's my favorite place."

He grins. "Mine, too."

It doesn't take long to get anywhere in Cunningham Falls, and before long we're seated at a table in the back corner. When the waitress arrives, she writes her name in crayon on the white paper covering the table.

"I'm Natasha," she says with a smile, "and I'll be helping you out tonight. Can I offer you some wine, or something else to drink?"

"Just a Coke for me," I reply.

"I'll have the same," Brad says. Natasha nods and bustles away and I turn my attention to the menu, even though I already know what I want.

I never change what I order here.

"What looks good?" I ask Brad and glance up to find him looking at me with heated green eyes.

"You look amazing."

"I meant the menu."

"I know what you meant," he says and tilts his head to the side, watching me. "Let's get this out of the way right now. What is it, exactly, that makes you nervous about me?"

I blink as Natasha places our Cokes in front of

us.

"Are you ready to order?"

"We need a minute," Brad says without looking away from me. He reaches out and takes my hand, and the same electricity hits me again, and I bite my lip. "Let's talk about this, Hannah."

"I'm not sure what to say."

"Is it the cop thing? My height? Have you heard something through the rumor mill?"

"What would I have heard?"

"Who knows?" He chuckles. "It's a small town."

I shrug. "Honestly, it's not *you* that makes me nervous. I'm not intimidated by you in the least."

"Excellent."

"I guess it's just first date jitters."

"Okay, we can work with that." He winks at me and nods at Natasha as she approaches the table. "I think we can order now."

"I'll have the bow-tie pasta with alfredo sauce, chicken, artichoke hearts, and mushrooms." I pass her the menu and smile at Brad.

"I'll have the lasagna," he says. Someone waves at him from across the room and he nods politely.

"It must be hard for you to be out in public when it's your day off."

He tilts his head in surprise. "What makes you

say that?"

"Well, I'm *always* on call. Babies don't know what office hours are. But you're the chief of police. People know you, and I'm sure they feel like they can approach you to ask questions, complain, what have you, no matter if you're on duty or not."

"Sometimes," he says with a nod. "I finally had to have my personal cell number changed because I kept getting calls. I have an official cell because I have to be able to be reached any time of day. But I don't need the townspeople to be able to call me whenever they see fit. I am a public servant, but I finally had to set some boundaries."

"Good for you," I reply. "Setting boundaries isn't easy."

"It is when an old lady calls you at two in the morning to complain about how bright her street light is. She doesn't like closing her blinds at night."

"Oh my."

"She wanted me to come out and unscrew the bulb in it so she could get some sleep."

I can't help but cover my mouth and laugh. "What did you tell her?"

"To close her damn blinds and I gave her the correct department to call the next day. She wasn't happy."

"I'm sorry," I say and lean back when our food is delivered. "It must be difficult to have a personal life when you're under a microscope."

"Not really," he says with a shrug and salts and peppers his food. "My father was the chief of police for about twenty years. He and my mom had a pretty normal life."

"Do they still live here?"

"Part time," he says with a nod. "They go south in the winter."

"I can't blame them for that. It was a snowy one this year."

He nods. "Where do your folks live?"

"My mom died when I was seventeen." I take a bite of food. "I have no idea where my dad is."

He's chewing and watching me. *Don't apologize.* That's the worst.

"That's tough," he says, surprising me. "Do you mind telling me what happened?"

"She and my dad were on their way home from a New Year's Eve party, and he hit a tree. Killed her instantly. He was incredibly intoxicated. It was my senior year of high school."

"Jesus."

"I miss her. She was a good mom, despite being married to an alcoholic. He was sent to prison for third degree manslaughter, but by the time he got out, I was long gone, in college. I've never seen or spoken to him since that day."

"You're quite nonchalant about it."

"I did the therapy thing, Brad. I've mourned. I still mourn her because she was wonderful. But he was a piece of shit, and I'm better off without him." I grab a piece of bread slathered in chunks of garlic and take a bite. "My aunt and uncle took me in for the rest of my senior year, and they've really become more like parents to me. Their daughter, Abby, has always been one of my best friends. I do have family."

"I'm glad," he replies. "Family is really important to me."

I nod. "I saw Jenna last night."

"She told me." He laughs and shakes his head, also taking a bit of bread. "She called this morning to tell me to be extra nice to you because she likes you."

"She's sweet."

"She's a meddler, but she's my only sister, and she tells me that's her job."

"And you have a younger brother as well, don't you?"

"Max," he says with a nod. "He's recently moved back to town as well. We're both busy, so I don't see him much, but it's good to have him nearby."

"That's how I feel about Drake."

"Drake Merritt?"

"Yes. He's one of my best friends. I met him in medical school."

"I thought for a while that he might be your boyfriend. That's why it took me so long to ask you out."

I feel my eyes widen in surprise. "Three years long? Brad, that's a long time. And no, he's never been my boyfriend. He's just a dear friend, and he's the reason I decided to move here."

"I'll have to thank him," Brad replies.

"You're quite charming." I sit back in my seat, stuffed full of pasta and bread, and cross my arms over my chest.

"Just honest." He finishes his food and wipes his mouth. "So, you have Drake and Grace nearby."

"I do. Grace is wonderful, and I still see her all the time, despite not being roommates anymore. And Abby and her family come to visit at the holidays."

"Is there anything else I can bring you?" Natasha asks as she comes to clear away our plates. "Dessert?"

"I mean, you can't come to Ciao and not get the tiramisu," I say and look to Brad for confirmation.

"We should absolutely share the tiramisu," he says with a nod.

Natasha leaves, but another person walks over to talk about the potholes in the street in front of their house, and how their neighbor keeps playing music late into the night.

Finally, after five minutes, Brad says, "I understand your frustration, Paul. Just give the city a call tomorrow and they'll talk to you about the potholes."

"What about the music?"

"You're always welcome to call the non-emer-gency line and an officer will come out and talk to them."

Paul grumbles, but walks back to his own table and Brad reaches around the untouched tiramisu to take my hand. "Sorry about that."

"Like I said before, I'm sure that happens all of the time when you're out on dates."

"I don't go out on many dates," he says with a smile.

"No?"

He shakes his head and passes me a clean fork, then loads his own fork with the fluffy dessert and offers me the bite.

Of course I take it, and close my eyes in abso-lute happiness as the coffee flavor hits my tongue.

"So damn good."

"Hannah," he says, his voice gruff. I open my eyes and meet his gaze. "You're so damn sexy."

"Enjoying dessert is sexy?"

"When you make those noises and close your eyes? Hell yes. Because I want to make you do those things for purely other carnal reasons."

I swallow hard and set my fork down, licking my lips. "Not tonight."

"Excuse me?"

"I'm not a sex on the first date kind of girl."

"I wasn't suggesting it," he says and takes another bite of dessert. "Doesn't make me want it any less."

We finish our meal, Brad pays the bill, and the next thing I know, we're on our way back to my place. It's after nine, but it's still light outside.

"I love summer," I say and roll my window down. "I love that it gets dark so late, and the warm weather. I always have the best of intentions to take a week off of work in the summer, just to enjoy it. But it never happens."

"I love it too. Do you ski?"

I laugh and shake my head. "No, I never have. We don't have mountains in Kansas, and since I've moved here, I've been too busy to ski. Also, I don't love to be cold."

"You live in Montana, sweetheart."

"Hey, I can stay inside where it's warm. I do, however, love to hike. I plan to go this weekend, in fact, barring any babies making their debut."

"I hike as well. I also love to boat, kayak, and ride my bike."

"You're outdoorsy." I turn in my seat so I can watch him as he drives. His jaw is square, his hands big and sure on the wheel. "Summers are so short here, I'd rather never go inside."

"Mind if I join you on your hike this weekend?"

I grin, enjoying the thought of hiking up the

mountain with Brad. "Of course. I was just going to walk to the top of the ski mountain."

"That's a four mile hike," he says with surprise.

"Too far for you?"

He glances at me, a small smile tugging his lips. "No, sweetheart, I was wondering if it's too far for *you.*"

"Psh, that's nothing."

He pulls up in front of my house, and I'm suddenly sad. I don't want to end the night yet.

"Do you watch Stranger Things?" I ask him.

"Yeah, I'm almost done with the first season."

"I'm halfway into the first season. If you don't mind rewatching a few episodes, would you like to come in and watch some of it with me?"

He immediately climbs out of the truck and around to open my door. "I'm in."

"I'm not getting naked," I remind him.

"So noted." He locks his truck and follows me to the door. "I also will not be getting naked."

Too bad.

I nod. "So noted."

CHAPTER THREE

Brad

HER HOUSE SMELLS JUST like her, like cinnamon and vanilla. Her red hair falls in loose curls around her shoulders as she leads me into her living room and queues up the TV, getting the next episode of the show ready.

"Do you want something to drink?" she asks. "I have Coke and bottled water. I might even have a Snapple if you want it."

"A water would be great."

She nods and hurries out of the room and back again, carrying two bottles of water. She's so full of nervous energy I want to pin her to the wall and kiss the fuck out of her, just to smooth out the nerves.

She passes me the water, and I set it on the coffee table, take hers from her and set it down as well, then take her hand in mine and pull her to me.

"Hannah."

"Yeah?" She looks up at me now, her big blue eyes wide. She licks her lower lip, and it's almost my undoing.

"You've got that nervous thing happening again."

"Oh." She clears her throat, and I draw her closer to me still. "I haven't had a man here in a long time." The words are a whisper and her eyes are pinned to my lips now.

"Good," I whisper in return and let my hands glide up her arms to her shoulders. "I'm going to kiss you."

"Okay."

I can't help but smile at the absolute eagerness in her voice, and the way she boosts herself up on her toes, getting ready for me.

God, she'd be so fucking responsive beneath me in bed.

But that's not for tonight. I push that thought from my brain and tilt my head down to hers, allowing my nose to brush back and forth against hers, enjoying the warmth of her skin close to mine and the way she takes a deep breath, making her chest rise.

"You're beautiful," I murmur against her lips.

"So are you," she replies. Her hands are moving over my shoulders and up into my hair, and I can't hold back any longer. I sink down into her, covering her mouth with mine, finally allowing myself to taste her, to soak her in. She's the sweetest thing I've ever seen, and her reaction to me is exactly what I imagined in my dreams.

She pushes up further on her toes, trying to get

closer to me, gripping the back of my hair tighter in her fists. My hands drift down to her ass and squeeze her firmly. She's pressed against me now, we're breathing heavily, and I have two choices: I either carry her to her bedroom, strip her naked, and fuck her into the mattress. Or, I stop this now because if I wait, I won't be able to stop.

And she already set the boundary of no sex tonight.

So, no sex it is.

"Hannah," I murmur and pull back, brushing my fingers through her hair. Her eyes are still closed and she's biting her lip. "Open your eyes, sweetheart."

"Hmm?" She complies, and then frowns. "We're stopping?"

"Oh yeah," I say with a nod and step away as soon as I'm sure she can stand under her own power. "If I don't stop now, I won't want to stop at all."

She seems to struggle with this information, but then sighs and nods. "Right. Sorry, Slutty Hannah took over there for a second."

"Don't do that." My voice is sharper than I intended, but the irritation is swift. "You're not a slut, Hannah. We're fucking attracted to each other. Jesus, the chemistry has been off the charts every time we're in the same room together since we first met. That's not being promiscuous."

"You're right. Again." She pushes her hair back. "If you want to go, I understand."

"Hell no, I want to watch this show." I sit in the middle of her couch so she has no choice but to sit next to me. "And I want to feel you next to me for a few hours."

She tilts her head, watching me for a moment, then shrugs and sits next to me after reaching for the remote. "Let me check my phone."

She pulls the device from her pocket, but there have been no calls.

"No babies so far tonight," she says with a grin. "I'm not expecting any of my patients to go into labor this week, actually, but you never know." She sets the phone aside and presses play on the show.

"Jenna said you got called out last night."

"Yeah, it was unexpected," she says and looks up at me with sad eyes. "The baby was stillborn. He was too premature, and we couldn't save him."

"I'm sorry."

"It happens."

"I'm sorry just the same," I reply and tug her against me. She fits perfectly in the crook of my shoulder, her head leaning on my chest.

"Shall we watch this?" she asks.

"Let's do it."

She snuggles up to me and we stay here, snuggled up together, as one episode, then another plays. Finally, she stretches and checks the time on her phone.

"I hate to kick you out, but I should get some

sleep. I have appointments first thing tomorrow."

"I have to be in the office early, too," I reply and stand. But rather than walk to the door, I pull her into my arms, hugging her tightly. I hold her for a long moment, then pull away and smile down at her.

"What was that for?" she asks.

"I needed it." *You needed it.* I wink and walk toward the front door. "When would you like to go for our hike?"

"Saturday morning," she says. "Before it gets crowded up there. I like to hike up and then ride the chairlift down."

"How does nine sound?"

"Perfect," she says with a nod. "It'll be fun."

"I think so, too."

I take one more long look at her, her blue eyes sleepy, her red hair mussed up now, and am already anticipating being with her on Saturday.

"Have a good night, Hannah."

"You too."

I walk to my truck, start the engine, and head toward home with the windows rolled down and my sunroof open. It's a warm night. There are a million stars in the sky, and I know if I drove up into Glacier National Park, just forty miles from here, I would be able to see the Milky Way.

That's something I can take Hannah to see another night.

Spending the evening with her was everything I'd hoped it would be. The chemistry is still there like a fucking freight train. It just rolls over us. But more than that, I enjoyed her company.

I plan to spend as much time with her as our schedules allow.

Once home, I secure my truck in the garage and walk into the house, greeted by my white lab, Sadie.

"Hey, girl." She whines a bit and presses her face into my hand, then goes directly to the back door, needing out. My back yard is fenced for her, so I let her out and walk through the house double checking locks and alarms. It's habit. I have to make sure the house and garage are always secure to protect myself from anyone who may be angry and want to take it out on the chief of police.

It happens.

Sadie scratches at the back door, and I let her in. We walk upstairs to the bedroom and she settles on her bed in the corner, ready for sleep.

But despite being tired, I'm restless. I take a long, hot shower which helps to calm me down. I slip into bed and think of a sexy redhead as I fall to sleep.

"Come in," I call when there's a knock on my office door. I've been doing paperwork all damn morning, and the distraction is welcome. I'm surprised when it's Max who walks through the door.

Sadie immediately jumps up from her bed by my desk to greet him.

"Hey, gorgeous girl," Max says and kneels to rub her head and give her kisses. "Aren't you the prettiest girl?"

Sadie falls on her back in elation, exposing her belly.

"You'd think she never gets any attention," I say and lean back in my chair. "Did you come to love on my dog?"

"Yes. And to see what you're up to."

"Just maintaining law and order," I reply. "What are *you* up to?"

"I have to go back to LA," he says with a frown. "I have some work that needs to be done in person."

Max is a highly successful software engineer. So successful that he's sold a few things to Google for a shit ton of money.

"How long will you be gone?"

"A month maybe," he says with a sigh. "Which sucks because this is my favorite time of year here."

"You don't have to work," I remind him. "You have more money than God."

"Probably not," he says with a laugh. "I mean, he's God. And maybe I don't have to work for the money, but I have to work for the sanity. What am I going to do, Brad, retire at thirty-two? And do what?"

"I don't know, it would drive me nuts too," I say and offer him a shrug. "When do you leave?"

"This afternoon."

I just raise an eyebrow, and he cringes. "I know, it's last minute. Jenna's dealing with the tree house architect. I was supposed to be there for the meeting, but I don't think she needs me. She's awesome at this, and can handle herself."

"Agreed," I reply. "Did you give her a heads up?"

"Yeah, and she said she'd be okay. But I told her to call you if she needs you."

"Okay, sounds good."

"Her meeting with them is Saturday morning. That's the only time they could meet this week."

"I'm not free Saturday morning," I reply.

"Why? Are you working?"

"No, I have a date."

He's quiet for a moment, and then he leans forward and I know I'm about to catch hell.

"With whom?"

"Hannah Malone."

"Nice. I like her."

"Do you know her?"

"It's a small town, big brother. Of course I know her. Not well, but she's hot as hell and seems nice."

"Don't make me break your arm again."

He smirks. "Don't worry, I'm not hot for her. Jenna probably won't need you, but if you could be in cell range just in case, I'd appreciate it."

"Not a problem," I reply and pet Sadie when she sits next to me and rests her head in my lap. "Need anything else?"

"Just keep an eye on my house for me."

"I'll have my guys drive by throughout the day."

"Thanks. I'll try to get home sooner. We'll see how it goes."

"Taking your jet?"

"Yeah, it's convenient." He watches me for a second and then smirks. "Hey, you're the one who said I have more money than God. What's the use if I don't spend some of it?"

"I didn't say anything," I insist. "Spend it all, I don't care."

"Let me pay off your house."

"Fuck you."

It's the same argument about every four months. Max wants to help. To share what he's built with those he loves, and I get that. But I don't need him to pay off my fucking house.

"This tree house project is going to cost you plenty."

"And I'll make the money back when Jenna

puts her magic on it," he replies with a nod. "Okay, I'll see you in a few weeks."

"See you."

He leaves my office, and I immediately call Jenna.

"Oh good, you called to tell me about your date."

"No, nosy girl, I called because Max just left my office. He's leaving for LA today."

"I know. I told him I'd get his mail for him."

"He said you have a meeting with the architect on Saturday?"

"Yeah, but I told him from the beginning that he didn't have to be there. This is a preliminary meeting where they'll show me what they have so far and I'll hate it, and then they'll have to rework it."

"You sound so optimistic." I smile and glance outside to see one of my officers talking to a kid with a skateboard. It's getting heated.

"It's just how it works. So it's really not a big deal that Max can't make it."

"I'll have my phone on me that morning, so just call if you need me."

"Yes, sir," she says, the way she does when she rolls her eyes at me. "Hi, I'm Jenna and I'm thirty-four years old. I've got this, Brad."

"Yeah, yeah. Call me if you need me."

I hang up on a deep sigh and stand to go to the window and watch the kid argue with my officer. Finally, the kid walks away, his skateboard under his arm. He turns back to flip the bird, and then jogs away.

My officer, Jacob, just hangs his head and sighs. Dealing with kids like that isn't fun, but Jacob is a good cop.

I glance back at my desk and frown at the paperwork I still have to do, then decide *fuck it.* I slip the leash on Sadie and walk out of my office.

"Patrice, we'll be back. I'm on my phone if you need me."

She just nods, not looking up from the computer. That's one of the things I like about Patrice; she doesn't say what isn't needed but she gets stuff done and doesn't take my crap.

This place wouldn't run without her.

It's another beautiful summer day, and sitting in my office isn't how I want to spend it. Sadie sits happily in my police-issue SUV passenger seat, her head out of the window letting the wind blow over her face.

I don't have a destination in mind, so I make a loop through town, passing by my place that sits near the lake, then up past Jenna's B&B and Max's house. The tourists haven't started to rush into town yet for the season, so the traffic isn't bad.

I head back through the older residential section of town, and past Hannah's house. I slow down because her front door is standing open, but I don't see a car in her driveway.

"Stay," I tell Sadie and walk to the door, my hand on my weapon. "Hannah?"

There's no answer. I walk around to the side of the house and look in a window, but I don't see anyone. I don't want to go in the house if she's there.

"Hannah," I call out again.

"Yeah?"

I spin around, caught off guard by the redhead herself who is sweaty and wearing little shorts and a tank top.

"Your front door is open."

"I know," she says and leans over to brace herself on her knees. "Good God, I hate to run."

"Why *were* you running?"

"I'm trying to get into summer shape," she says. "I'm super lazy in the winter." She swallows hard. "I mean, it's cold and I don't like that."

"Yes, you mentioned that last night."

She nods, still catching her breath. "But I love to be active in the summer, and I'm trying to get in shape for it."

"Why was your door open?"

"Because I forgot to shut it," she says with a shrug. "I ran in really fast to use the bathroom because all that running made me have to *go*."

I grin and cross my arms over my chest.

"You look really intimidating with that whole cop stance you have going on there."

"I'm on duty," I remind her.

"Yeah. It's hot." She grins. "Am I allowed to flirt with you when you're on duty, or is that too cliché?"

"You can flirt with me any time you like."

She laughs and wipes the sweat from her forehead with the back of her hand. Sadie lets out a bark and whimper, reminding me that she's there.

"Who's this?"

"Sadie," I reply and walk ahead of Hannah so I can let Sadie out of the vehicle.

"Can I pet her?"

"She'll be disappointed if you don't."

"Hi, Sadie," Hannah says and holds her hand out for the dog to smell. "You're so pretty. What a good girl you are. You're so brave, too."

And just like that, Sadie is nuzzling Hannah's leg and soaking up the attention.

"I didn't know you have a police dog."

"She's a retired police dog. I bring her with me when I'm going to be in my office most of the day."

"What brought you by my house?" she asks.

"I needed to get out of the office for awhile, so I thought I'd drive by here to make sure everything was okay."

"And my door was open."

I nod and watch as she continues to pet Sadie's head, putting the dog into a happiness coma.

"Thanks for checking on me. It was a bathroom emergency."

"Why aren't you in the office today?"

"I had morning appointments," she says with a smile. "I take one afternoon and two mornings off during the week because I inevitably end up working several evenings and weekends throughout the month. It all comes out in the wash, and I can catch up on sleep if I need it."

"I see. Well, we'll let you get back to your workout."

"Oh, I'm done. I'll be good until Saturday." She sits on the ground and lets Sadie fall into her lap. "This is the sweetest dog ever."

"And she knows it." I check the time, and then hear my radio go off in the car. "Hold on."

I jog over and listen to a report of an accident just south of town. Multiple cars, injuries.

"I have to go. There's been an accident." I stare at Sadie. "Damn it, I shouldn't have brought her along."

"Leave her with me," Hannah offers. "We'll hang out for a couple of hours."

"You don't have to—"

"Go," Hannah says. "I have this. Be safe."

I nod and hurry away, my head already in the accident scene I'm rushing to.

CHAPTER FOUR

Hannah

|DIDN'T SLEEP. NOT MUCH, anyway. One of my colleagues was out of town yesterday, and of course that's when two of his patients decided to go into labor. I was at the hospital late into the night.

I should call Brad and tell him that I'll have to take a rain check on the hike today. That's the responsible thing to do. I should sleep. If a bear runs out onto the trail and tries to kill me, I'm way too tired to run away.

I'm just trying to save my own life here.

I roll my eyes and stare at myself in the mirror.

"You don't want to cancel. You like him. Not to mention, his dog is the cutest ever."

Sadie is maybe the sweetest dog I've ever met. She hung out with me all afternoon the other day, following me around the house and then jumping up on the bed with me and sleeping until Brad came to pick her up.

Maybe I should get a dog.

My doorbell rings just as I finish tying my hiking shoes, and I rush out to open the door, only to stop dead in my tracks and stare in the rudest way possible at the man standing in front of me.

He's not wearing sleeves. So, his muscles are just hanging out all over the place. And dear God, the muscles! He could probably just lift me over his head.

It's almost ridiculous.

"Hi," he says with a grin and holds a to-go cup from Sips out for me. "This is for you."

"Oh, thanks." I take a sip and feel my eyes go wide. "This is exactly the drink I always order."

"I know," he says with a grin. "I asked them to make your usual."

"Are you real?"

"Excuse me?"

"I mean, you have the sweetest dog ever, you bring me coffee, and have you *seen* you?"

He laughs now and leans in to kiss my forehead. "You look tired."

"I didn't sleep much."

"We don't have to go."

"Oh yes we do," I reply and back away from him before I humiliate myself and jump him here in my living room. "I have to go."

"Why?"

I just shake my head and grab my backpack. I have fresh water in the bladder, a few packs of jerky and nuts, and my bear spray, which I check twice.

"You probably won't need the spray."

"We have the highest concentration of grizzly bears in the lower 48 states," I inform him and feel my heart already pick up speed at the thought. "I need the spray."

"I just mean that I'm always carrying, so if something happens, we'll be safe."

I stop and glance at him. "You always carry a gun?"

"Yes, ma'am."

"Why?"

"I'm the police chief. You never know what might happen."

"Huh." I shrug, but keep the bear spray where it is, reach for my coffee, and lead Brad out of my house. "You brought her!"

I hurry to the truck, toss my bag in the back seat, and hug the beautiful Sadie.

"She got a warmer hello than I did," he says when he gets into the truck and starts the engine.

"We're friends," I inform him and kiss Sadie's cheek. She's grinning.

"You and I aren't friends?"

"Are you really jealous of your dog?"

"Never thought I would be," he mumbles and pulls away from my house, making me smile.

"Thank you for the coffee." I reach out and touch his thigh, feeling the way his muscles tighten up at my touch. I'm relieved that it's not just me. That I'm not the only one who tenses up when we're together.

The things this man does to my body are ridiculous, considering we've never been naked together.

"When was the last time you did this hike?" he asks me.

"Last fall," I reply. "You?"

"Oh geez, it's been a long time. I was probably in high school."

"Cool." I grin at him and sip my coffee. "It'll be new for you then."

We're soon parked near the bottom of the chair lift. There's a whole village up here of uber-expensive homes, condos, and the ski village itself with a lodge and small convenience store. Almost everything has begun to open up again for the summer tourist season, when people will come up here to hike, bike, zip line, and a whole bunch of other outdoor activities. But it's still early in the season.

That doesn't mean the trail isn't busy. The locals love the outdoors, too, so we won't be alone on the trail, which makes me feel better.

The more people there are, the fewer the bears.

Once we have our backpacks on and Sadie is

on her leash, we set off to the trail head, which is just about a hundred yards from the chair lift. It's not an easy climb. Four miles of walking steadily uphill is strenuous, but it's also incredibly beautiful.

We climb out of some trees and onto one of the ski runs, currently covered in grass and flowers, and take a moment to look down onto the valley below.

"Holy shit," Brad murmurs. We stand side by side and take it all in. We can see about fifty miles south, over three different towns. And to the west is Glacier National Park, which we'll be able to see even better from the top.

"It's stunning, isn't it?"

"That's a good word for it," he replies, looking down at me. "How did I forget about this?"

"I think we often take what's in our backyard for granted," I reply as we begin to walk on the trail again. We walk over a log bridge that covers a rushing creek, the water high with snow run-off.

My heart is beating at a ludicrous pace. It's dumb, I'm not going to die on this mountain, but I can't help it. I'm terrified.

"How are you doing?" Brad asks.

"I'm fine," I reply. The hike isn't taxing me at all. I reach down and feel the bear spray on my hip, which makes me feel a bit better.

"That's the fourth time you've reached for that bear spray, and we're not even a mile up yet."

"It's habit," I say. "You know, you don't have to follow me. I can walk behind you."

"Not a chance," he says and I roll my eyes so he can't see.

"Are you trying to be chivalrous?"

"I'm learning you," he replies. "Tell me about this bear phobia."

"Why do you think that?"

"Because you just reached for the spray again."

My heart is hammering, and I can't stop looking around me, listening for any tiny sound. We've passed several people hiking down. They're the go-getters, who come up here super early, hike up, and then have to hike back down because the chair lifts aren't running yet.

I'm not quite that ambitious.

And not one of them was running down the trail for their lives.

"I do have a bear thing. I'm absolutely terrified," I admit and feel my throat burn with tears that want to come, but I swallow hard. I will *not* cry over a fucking bear that isn't even here.

"Why?"

"Because we have the highest concentr—"

"Yes, I know that part," he says.

"Every summer since I've lived here, at least one person has died from a bear attack. Two were injured last year. They love the huckleberries, and there are berries all over this mountainside."

"Then why hike here?"

"Because I love it." I shrug and then shake my head, laughing at myself. "Maybe I have this stupid thought in my head that if I face the fear, I can make it go away. But so far, it isn't working."

"I've never responded to a grizzly fatality on this mountain."

"So you weren't there when that poor man and his daughter were attacked last year?"

"Neither of them died."

I stop and turn around, petting Sadie when she leans on my knee. "You're missing the point, Brad. It's an irrational fear for you. You have a weapon and you know how to use it. You also have Sadie, who I'm sure would go ballistic if a bear was nearby.

"I'm just me." I hold my hands out to my side. "Me and bear spray. But damn it, I live in this beautiful place, and I'll be damned if I won't explore it once in a while. My anxiety can bite me."

"Good girl," he says with a smile. I don't respond, I just turn to keep walking, but just then a cyclist coming downhill way too fast turns the corner and bumps me, hard. "Hannah!" Brad yells, as I stumble down the side of the goddamn mountain, stopping myself on a tree trunk.

"Ouch." I cringe and brush some leaves some my hair.

"Are you okay?" he says from beside me, bracing himself on the tree, digging his feet in so he doesn't slide down the mountainside, and assessing the damage. Sadie is with him, whimpering.

"Is she sad?"

"She wants to work," he says. "She's waiting for commands."

"What a good girl."

"Are you okay?" he asks again.

"My ankle hurts." I take a deep breath, trying to keep my anxiety at bay. "It's probably just a sprain."

Or, you know, broken.

It's not broken.

Except, what if it *is* broken? I'm on a fucking mountain and my ankle could be broken.

Shit. Shit shit shit.

"Let's get back up to the trail." Brad takes my hand and helps me to my feet. I refuse to put any weight on my hurt ankle, so I'm horribly off balance. "How bad is the ankle?"

"How am I supposed to know?"

His lips twitch. "You're a doctor, sweetheart."

"Oh. Right." I glance up the hill and feel my eyes widen. "Holy fuck, did I fall that far?"

"You did," he says grimly. "And we're going to get you back up there."

"Oh my God. Brad, if this is broken, I won't

be able to get up there. I'll be stuck here. I'll die." I reach for my bear spray, but it's gone, probably unclipped from my backpack in the fall.

And just like that, hysterics decide to set in.

"Hey," Brad says, but I don't hear him. I can't breathe.

I'm going to die on this damn mountain.

Why didn't I stay home?

The next thing I know, Brad has slung me over his shoulder, and he is carrying me back up to the trail, where he finds a tree stump and sits me on it.

"Hannah."

I'm breathing too hard to reply. Sadie lays her head on my lap, but rather than finding it sweet, I want to push her away.

I want to push *him* away.

"Hannah." He takes my face in his hands and makes me look at him. "Listen to my voice. Just listen to me."

"Bear spray," I manage, but he shakes his head.

"Shh. Listen to me. Hannah, you're okay. I'm not going to let anything happen to you. No bear is going to get you."

"I'm dumb."

"No." He wipes his thumbs over my cheeks and continues to talk so soothingly. "I need to know how bad that ankle is."

I shake my head and lean on his shoulder,

breathing deeply and fundamentally mortified.

This is not how I planned to spend date number two.

"Can you put your weight on it for me?"

"No."

He leans in and presses his lips to my ear, erasing all thought of my ankle.

"Hannah, you're badass. I know you had a bad moment down there, but you've got this."

His hands are rubbing up and down my arms, and I take a long, deep breath. He's right, I do have this, and it's because just being with him and listening to his voice has calmed me, which is new.

I pick my head up and look him dead in the eye, then plant my sore foot on the ground and stand.

"It's not broken."

"Good." He's still touching me, grounding me. "Can you get down the mountain?"

"I can get *up* the goddamn mountain," I reply and raise my chin. "I'm sorry you saw that."

"Don't be." He gives Sadie a hand gesture and the dog falls into line next to him. "We can go down to the car."

"I came to hike." I step away from him and cringe inside when there's a slight twinge in my ankle. But it's not broken, or even sprained.

"I don't want you to hurt yourself."

"I'll take it easy." I look back at him and offer

him a smile. "Honest, I want to hike this mountain. I'll take it slow, and I've got you with me, so I'm safe from bears, right?"

He tilts his head to the side, and I can see the wheels turning in his head. I'm sure he's wondering if he should make me go back.

I mean, he could try.

"You're safe," he confirms.

"Great, let's walk up this mountain."

"It never gets old," I say and take a long, deep pull of the fresh mountain air. "I mean, look at these mountains."

"You're right," he says and takes a drink of water, then pulls a bowl out of his pack and pours some water for Sadie, who eagerly drinks it down. "This was worth the four miles."

"Right?" I turn to him, excited. The wooden platform we're standing on is at the summit of the mountain, and we're looking into Glacier National Park and on into Canada.

It feels like we're at the top of the world.

Brad drags a finger down my cheek and hooks a stray piece of hair over my ear. "How's your ankle?"

"Fine." Sore. Swollen.

He leans in and presses those lips to my ear

again. "You don't ever lie to me, Hannah. I thought we already had that worked out."

"It's sore."

He kisses my cheek. "Let me take you home and put your feet up."

I back up an inch and raise an eyebrow at him. "To your house?"

"My house."

"You want to take care of my sore ankle."

"I want to be with you. I don't give a rat's ass in what capacity that is. Hiking, grocery shopping, watching TV, or having you naked and moaning under me."

He's still whispering, but he makes me blush.

"Okay."

"To what?"

"Your house."

He grins and kisses me chastely, then motions for Sadie to come to the chairlift line with us. Because we have her with us, we have to ride in a gondola, rather than on the chair, which is fine with me.

The view is the same.

I press my face to the window and watch the valley coming closer and closer. We pass over people hiking the trail. A deer and her fawn are lazily eating in a meadow.

"I wonder who that kid was that tried to kill

me?" I wonder out loud.

"He was going too fast for me to see," Brad replies grimly. "He did yell *sorry*."

"Well, that's something."

We come to a stop at the bottom of the lift, and I hobble out of the gondola. Sitting for only twenty minutes has made the ankle swell more and get stiff.

Damn it.

We begin to walk to the truck, but Brad stops me. "Wait here, I'll go get the truck."

"You can't drive back here."

A cocky smile slides over his lips. "Honey, I can drive wherever I want. And you're injured. Sadie, stay with Hannah."

Sadie sits at my side and we wait while Brad, still wearing the sleeveless shirt, jogs to the truck and returns with it a few minutes later.

He helps me inside, and begins the descent down the mountain.

"I live not too far away," he informs me. "We'll get some ice on the ankle."

"It's too nice outside to spend it indoors," I reply with a slight pout. "Dumb ankle."

He smiles. "I think we can work something out."

He's right, it doesn't take us long to get down the mountain and to his house. He has a nice sized lot with a tall white fence surrounding it. The house is grey and not too big. Well cared for, and new.

"Did you have this built?"

"Yeah, about three years ago," he says as he pulls into the garage, cuts the engine, and closes the door behind us. "Stay here for a minute."

It's not a question, and he doesn't give me time to ask why. He's out of the truck, along with Sadie, and inside before I can blink. I'm waiting for maybe five minutes when he comes back into the garage and opens the door for me.

"Sorry about that, I wanted to make sure everything was still locked up tight and there was no danger before you came in."

"Why do I think there's a story behind that statement?"

He shrugs and takes my hand, helping me out of the tall truck. When I limp inside his house, he simply lifts me into his arms and walks into the kitchen.

"How about a tour?"

"Are you going to carry me through the whole house?"

"I hope so."

I laugh and nod. "Okay. Give me the grand tour."

There's a white and gleaming stainless steel kitchen, living room, and three bedrooms, one of which has been made into an office. The master bedroom is spacious enough for his king bed, a dog bed for Sadie, and a sitting area. French doors open to a patio in the backyard.

The master bath is what dreams are made of with marble floors and countertops. There's a huge walk-in shower, and a large, free-standing soaking tub.

"I could swim in that tub."

"Be nice and you might get the chance," he says with a wink. He carries me back to the living area, but rather than set me on the couch, he walks out of another large set of French doors to the backyard, and my mouth drops.

"Okay, this is my favorite part of the house."

"Mine, too," he says with a grin and lowers me to an outdoor sofa. He kisses my forehead, then turns and walks back into the house.

The patio is covered, with a fireplace in the corner. It's truly an outdoor living space, with plush cushions and a dining room table, along with a grill and outdoor kitchen on the opposite side.

A waterfall runs behind me, making me sleepy.

"Did you do all of this landscaping yourself?" I ask when he returns with a towel and a bag of ice.

"Most of it," he says. "Jenna helped some. She has the green thumb. I like to be outside in the summer, and I wanted a beautiful outdoor space."

"Well, you got it." He rests my foot in his lap and covers it with the towel and ice. "Oh, that's good."

"You probably shouldn't have hiked the rest of the mountain."

"I'm going to be fine," I assure him. "I'll rest for the weekend, and be good as new in a couple of days."

"Have you always had anxiety?" he asks, throwing me off.

"For as long as I can remember." I nod, keeping my eyes on my foot. We said we'd always tell the truth. "I can remember waking up in the middle of the night as a little girl and needing to throw up. I wasn't sick. And once I did that, I'd go back to sleep and feel better.

"My dad wasn't mean. But he liked to drink, quite a lot actually. No one likes to be around a drunk, even if he is happy go lucky."

"No, they don't."

"I used to call it stress. I can stress out about stress that hasn't happened yet. I over think. I imagine the worst."

I always think that I'm going to die.

"But sometimes, it'll just come out of the blue, and I freak out. It doesn't last long. Are you scared off yet?"

"Should I be?"

"I'm a mess, Brad. I worry about things that aren't happening."

"You're not a mess. You have anxiety."

"Yeah, well, sometimes it feels like they're one and the same. So if you want to take me home and forget all about this, I'd understand."

"I'm a cop," he says and massages my calf. "I work *all the time*. I see shit that no one should ever see, even in a small town. I've been known to have an occasional night terror. I'm not prince charming, Hannah. We all have shit that we're dealing with."

"Yeah. We do." I reach out and take his hand in mine, squeezing it hard. "I'm sorry."

"I'm okay," he says. "It could be a lot worse."

"Do you have night terrors all the time?"

"No, but often enough. You should know that if we move forward because I don't want to scare the piss out of you. I'll never hurt you. But I might yell. Get restless."

"What helps?"

He stops and looks at me as if he's confused.

"What helps calm you down?"

"I don't know."

I nod, understanding completely. Until this afternoon, I didn't know either.

"So, the same goes," he continues. "If you'd like to go, I get it."

"I can't walk very far," I reply. But I let the ice fall to the floor and scoot into his lap, wrapping my arms around his neck. "I'm not going."

"Thank Christ."

CHAPTER FIVE

Brad

IT'S THE END OF the work day and I'm ready to head out. I have a date with Hannah that I've been looking forward to all day, but just as I'm about to reach for my keys, I get a call on the work cell.

I send it to voice mail.

And then twenty seconds later, I get a call on my personal cell.

"Hell," I mutter and answer.

"I know you're done for the day, Chief, but I think you're going to want to know about this," Officer Thomas, a long time friend and cop says.

"What's up?"

"I need you to come down to the city beach."

"I'll be there in ten."

I hang up and hurry out to the truck, calling Hannah on my way.

"Hey there," she says with a smile in her voice.

"I might be a little late," I say. "I'm sorry, I just

got a call."

"If anyone understands, it's me. Just keep me posted. Do you want me to go look in on Sadie?"

I grin, wondering how in the hell I got lucky enough to find this sweet woman. "She'll be okay. She was with me until lunch time."

"Sounds good. Be safe."

She hangs up just as I'm getting close to the city beach, or the swimming area at the head of our lake where people can swim and launch their boats.

There's an ambulance, two squad cars, a fire truck, and a crowd gathered around one of the boat launch docks.

"What's going on?" I ask Thomas as I approach. "And why are these people standing around?"

"We haven't had time to shoo them off," he says with a grim frown. "It's bad, Chief." He leads me to the ambulance, which is angled away from the onlookers. Sam Waters, the head EMT with the department is standing inside next to a gurney with a body covered with a sheet.

"Chief," Sam says. "We worked on him for thirty minutes, but there was nothing we could do."

"Why aren't you on the way to the hospital?"

"He won't be going to the hospital," Sam says. "You didn't hear the call?"

"No, I turned the scanner down while I finished some paperwork. Who is this?"

Sam and Thomas share a look.

"Who the fuck is it?"

"Kendall Reardon," Sam says and rubs his fingers over his mouth. "Kyle's oldest."

"Fuck," I mutter and dig my thumb and forefinger into my eyes. "How?"

"From what we can tell, he dove into the water from a boat and was electrocuted."

"What?" My head whips up.

"There was an underground electric box that surfaced, and it killed him."

"No more swimming." I yell over at the other officers who are managing crowd control. "Teller! No more swimming or boating until we get this figured out. Get all of the boats off this lake, and I want a team patrolling to make sure no one is swimming. Have the owner of the boat take you to where this happened, and call the damn electric company to get this taken care of."

"Yes, Chief," Dan Teller says and moves into action. I get on the radio and call in all of the men I have that are currently off duty. I need all hands on deck for this.

"I didn't think you'd want just anyone to talk to Kyle," Thomas says. "I know you guys go way back."

"You're right." I nod and make another call for my chaplain. "Get Kendall to the morgue, and make sure no one sets foot in that water."

"Yes, sir," both Sam and Thomas reply at the

same time. I run to my truck and take a call from the chaplain on duty.

"What's going on?" Matt Nichols asks. He's been a chaplain for five years, but he's lived in Cunningham Falls all of his life.

"We need to visit Kyle Reardon," I reply before clearing my throat. "Kendall was killed this afternoon."

"Damn," Matt mutters. "Is he home this time of day?"

"I fucking hope so, because I don't want to have to go to the school to deliver this news. School just got out for the summer, so the chances are good he'll be home. Meet me at his place and we'll go from there. I want to get to him before someone else calls him."

We hang up and I'm at Kyle's house within five minutes. Matt pulls up right behind me. I take a deep breath and stare at the small, well kept house that I've spent many mornings in having coffee with my friend after his kids have gone off to school. Kyle lost his wife to cancer just a couple of years ago, and now I have to deliver the news that his oldest son isn't coming home.

Matt waits for me on the sidewalk, and I join him, then walk with him to the door. Kyle's car is in the driveway.

He's home. He opens the door, and the second he sees both me and Matt, his eyes fill with sadness and he gestures for us to come inside.

I should go home. I should absolutely *not* go to Hannah's tonight. My emotions are raw. I would not be good company right now. But I can't seem to stay away. I shoot her a quick text and ask her if it's too late to drop by, and she immediately answers not at all.

Kyle only lives about four blocks from her, so I'm there quickly. She answers the door with a sunny smile, lifting my heavy heart just a bit.

"I'm so glad you texted," she says as she steps back, letting me inside.

"I shouldn't have," I reply honestly and shove my hand in my hair, pacing her living room. "I should have gone home."

She cocks her head to the side and props her hands on her hips. She's in shorts and a simple T-shirt, but I've never seen anything so beautiful in all of my life.

"Why didn't you?"

"Go home?" She nods. "Hell, because I'm not good company for myself either, and being with you sounded much better than pacing my house while Sadie watches with sad eyes."

"Why are you upset?"

I rub my fingers over my lips, not wanting to put what I did today in her head.

"Dead babies," she says and walks right to me, wrapping her arms around my waist and looking up at me with shining blue eyes. "I deliver dead babies. I have to tell women that they have cancer. Or that their child will have Down's syndrome. Or a deformity. I have had a twelve year old girl in my office, pregnant, and terrified to tell her parents.

"I can take this. I can hear whatever it is that you have to unload."

I drag my fingers down her soft cheek and enjoy the way her arms feel around me, then take a deep breath.

"Do you know Kyle Reardon?"

She frowns. "The principal?"

"Yes."

"I don't think I've met him personally, but Grace has always had nice things to say about him."

"His oldest son died today."

The words sound hollow to my own ears.

"Oh, Brad."

"Seventeen years old," I continue and pull away from her. Not because I don't love her touch, but because I have to pace. If I'm going to tell this, I don't want her to touch me until it's over.

"I've known Kyle all of my life. He was a little older than me in school, but we're friends. We ski together in the winter. I've known all of his kids since they were born, and I mourned with him when he lost his wife two years ago to cancer."

"Oh no," she says, but I keep talking.

"And today, I had to show up at his doorstep

with a chaplain and explain to him that his son was electrocuted in the water and was killed instantly. That there was nothing *anyone* could do, and that it wasn't anyone's fault. It was a stupid, horrible accident, and it took his son's life."

"I'm so sorry."

"Before I could tell him *anything*, I had to call his sister to come get his other three children, and then I held him while he wept. My friend, who has been through hell and back in the past few years, and was finally pulling it back together. How do you do that?"

I stop and narrow my eyes, barely seeing her now, lost in my own head. "How do you do that, Hannah?"

"You just do," she says softly. "You do what you have to do, and you're strong for them, and then you go home and you fall apart."

"It's so fucking unfair," I growl and shake my head. "Kendall was going to be a senior this year, and he was a phenomenal football player. And not just for a small town. For any town."

"He sounds like a special kid."

I nod and swallow hard, trying to keep it together. "He is. Was."

"Do you need to go be with Kyle?"

"Not tonight. We stayed for a couple of hours, and then his sister and mom came back with the kids. There will be visitors and lots of food delivered when news spreads through town, as it always does. I was so damn worried that someone who was at the lake would call him before I got to him."

"They didn't?"

"His phone started ringing just as I walked in the door, and I told him to turn it off." I shake my head again, still not fully grasping it all.

And Hannah walks back into my arms again, hugging me fiercely, her face pressed to my chest. I hug her back, holding her tightly, and bury my nose in her hair, breathing her in. She's the calm in the storm for me.

"Thank you for listening," I murmur. She tilts her head up, and I want to kiss the fuck out of her. I want to haul her to her bedroom and strip her bare and have my way with her until we've both forgotten our names.

But not tonight. My emotions are raw, and I refuse the first time I sink inside her to be when I'm upset.

"I have an idea," she says, oblivious to my thoughts.

"What's that?"

"How about ice cream?"

I frown down at her, thrown off course. "What about it?"

"It always makes me feel better. Let's walk down to the ice cream place and get a scoop."

"We could drive."

She shakes her head and pulls away. She shoves

a twenty-dollar bill in her pocket along with her keys and pulls her hair up in a messy ponytail. "It's a beautiful evening. Let's walk. It's less than half a mile."

"How do you know that?"

"Oh, I checked. If I walk, I can get two scoops." Her blue eyes are still full of worry, but she's trying to take my head out of the horror of today, and damn if it isn't working.

After a couple of blocks of walking on the uneven sidewalks, the trees above us on the boulevards swaying in the slight early summer breeze, I pull her hand up to my lips and kiss her knuckles.

"You're right. It's a beautiful night."

"I know." She grins. "This place changes out the flavors all the time. Maybe they have some summer flavors."

"You're really serious about your ice cream."

She laughs. "Ice cream is serious business."

It's past seven in the evening, so there's a line, but we wait patiently, reading the board of flavors. When it's our turn, Hannah gets a scoop of huckleberry and a scoop of cinnamon vanilla, surprising me when she passes on the coffee ice cream.

It all sounds great, but I get the same as Hannah and before I know it, we're on our way back to her house. Our steps are slower this time, as we eat and enjoy the evening.

"Wait. Did you pay for my ice cream?" I stop

and stare down at her in surprise.

"Sure did."

"Not cool, Doctor Malone."

"Why, Chief Hull? A girl can't buy a guy ice cream?"

"Not this guy. If we're on a date, I'm paying."

"That's quite chivalrous, and cave man, of you," she says with a laugh. "I'm happy to splurge on some ice cream once in a while. I promise not to make a habit out of it."

"Now you're mocking me."

I take the last bite of my cone and wipe my mouth with the napkin.

"Of course I am," she agrees. "You're being ridiculous."

"It's ridiculous for a man to take care of his woman?"

This makes her pause, as she eats the last of her ice cream as well, and then tucks her napkin in her back pocket.

"A couple of things," she says at last. "First, I can, and do, take care of myself."

"And what's the other thing?"

"Who says I'm your *woman*?"

"Me." We stop on the sidewalk and I turn her to face me, my hands gripping her shoulders. "I'm sure as fuck not sharing you with anyone."

"Well, I didn't suggest that either," she says,

shaking her head, then continues walking. About ten feet away, she looks back at me over her shoulder. "Are you coming?"

"That's all you have to say?"

"You answered my question. But you need to know that I'm an independent woman, Brad. Not because I'm trying to prove anything to anyone, but because that's just who I am. I don't need to be saved."

"Not trying to save you," I reply reasonably. I've never wanted to fuck anyone so bad in my life. "Just letting you know that when we're together, I'll be buying you dinner."

"And dessert, apparently."

We've arrived at her house, but I don't follow her up to her door. She walks back down to the bottom of the steps. "You don't want to come in?"

"I do." I cup her cheek and she leans into my touch. "So I'd better not."

She looks disappointed, but nods. "I don't have to be at the clinic until noon tomorrow," she informs me. "In case you need anything."

I lean in and cover her lips with mine, tasting the sweetness from the huckleberries and the cinnamon she just ate. Tasting *her.*

"Have a good night," I murmur against her lips and turn to leave.

When I start my truck and drive away, she's still standing on her sidewalk, her fingers on her lips, watching me go.

I'm in the water. I'm an excellent swimmer, but I can't move. It's like I'm trudging through wet cement. My legs are heavy, and I can't get through the water fast enough.

I look up and see Kendall floating in the water, face down, just twenty feet away from me. If I can just get over to him, I might be able to save him. What's he doing in the water?

Suddenly, I'm surrounded by floating bodies. My men. My sister and brother. Hannah. All just out of my reach.

I can't save them.

The water is rising around me, no longer just around my legs, but up to my chest now. Then my chin, and over my head.

I'm completely submerged, my feet still held in the bottom of the lake. I look up and see faces staring down at me. Faces of those I love. Their eyes are wide open, glaring at me in accusation.

You didn't even try to save us.

I'm fighting to swim. To dislodge my feet, but it's no use. I can't get free.

I wake up, sitting the bed, screaming. I'm covered in sweat, and Sadie is standing beside me, whining in worry.

I still can't breathe. I tip my face up, gasping for air and trying to push the terror away.

I haven't had an episode like this in over a year, but it's not surprising after yesterday. The sadness is here again, but the guilt is gone.

There was nothing I could do about what happened. I couldn't save him.

But my friend is hurting, and that makes me sad. A kid who had a bright future ahead of him is gone, and that's the biggest tragedy of all.

I push my hands through my soaked hair, then pat the bed, inviting Sadie up. She's not usually allowed on the bed, but I could use some companionship right now, and Hannah is clear across town.

Hannah.

She calmed me down yesterday. She seemed to understand, and I don't think I've ever known anyone except my dad who could really understand what this part of the job is like.

She's a special woman, and now that I have her in my life, I'm not going to fuck it up.

Sadie finally lays her head down to sleep, and I leave the bed for a shower. I'm gross, as if I'd been in the ring at the gym for an hour. Once clean, I put on clothes for the day and brew a cup of coffee.

It's only four in the morning, but I'm up for the day. I'll never go back to sleep now.

I want to go to Hannah's and climb into bed with her, but she's asleep, and we aren't quite there yet. Soon, I hope.

Sadie pads out of the bedroom, her eyes sleepy.

"You don't have to get up," I tell her, but she

sits next to me, always loyal. I let her outside and set some food down for her, which she appreciates when she comes back in. Finally, I sit in my living room with another cup of coffee and Sadie at my feet and wait for morning.

Four hours later, I walk into Drips & Sips and nod at Anna, the owner who happens to be working behind the counter today.

"Are you taking coffee to a certain doctor again today?" she asks. Anna might be the nosiest person in town, which is saying a lot because Cunningham Falls has its share of nosy people.

"I am," I reply with a nod. "And I'll take my usual as well."

She gets busy making our drinks.

"Heard about that poor Reardon boy," Anna says, shaking her head. "Do you have anything you can tell me?"

"No, ma'am," I reply and grit my teeth. "It's an ongoing investigation."

"It's just so horrible. Poor Kyle. He must just be devastated."

"I'm sure." *Just make the fucking coffee.*

Anna keeps chirping about Kendall and his mom, then finally passes the coffees to me, which I throw a bill down for and tell her to keep the change, just wanting to get the hell out of here.

Sadie is waiting patiently for me in the car. When I turn down Hannah's street, Sadie gets excited. She already knows where Hannah's house is.

Seems I'm not the only one falling for her.

CHAPTER SIX

Hannah

SOMEONE IS RINGING MY fucking doorbell. I was at the hospital until the wee hours, I was finally in a deep, lovely sleep, and someone is ringing the bell.

All I know for sure is, this had better not be the damn door-to-door people trying to sell me a vacuum. Or a magazine. Or Jesus.

I wrap my robe around me, stumbling toward the door. I pull it open and am surprised to find an excited Sadie and a ridiculously sexy Brad standing at my door.

"Is that coffee?" I ask.

"For you," he confirms and holds it out to me.

"Come to mama," I mutter and take it from his hand, taking a grateful sip. Sadie brushes past my leg, into the house, and curls up on my couch.

"She's not supposed to be on the furniture," Brad says.

"My house, my rules," I reply and take another sip of the one thing in this world I'm addicted to, and give him a once over from head to toe. "You look like you got about as much sleep as I did."

"Rough night?" he asks without confirming or denying.

"Babies," I reply with a shrug. "You?"

He just shrugs. "Are you going to ask me in?"

"Sure." I back up and gesture him into the room. "Sorry, I was sleeping pretty good. My energy level is about equal to a sloth on Xanax."

"I can leave and let you go back to bed."

His eyes roam up and down my body, reminding me that I'm just in a robe and nothing else. His green eyes are hot, and every muscle in his body is tight.

Even sleep deprived, I can tell when a man is in the mood.

"You've brought me coffee. I'll never kick you out when you've done that."

"I'll remember that," he says with a chuckle.

"Besides, I have plenty of room." I turn and walk into my bedroom, glancing behind me to see that he's following me. He makes a hand gesture at Sadie, which I assume means *stay*. "We can take a nap," I suggest.

His lips twitch, but he doesn't say anything when he joins me next to the bed. He takes my coffee and sets both of our cups on the bedside table.

"Is that what you want, Hannah?" he murmurs and skims his fingertips down my arms.

"Eventually."

He hitches his finger in the belt of my robe. "What do you have on under here?"

I'm staring at his mouth. His lips are just… *wow.* I want them on me. All over me. Every fucking inch.

"Maybe you should just take it off and find out," I whisper, unsure of where my voice went.

He takes a long, deep breath, his finger is moving back and forth under the belt. He leans in and kisses my forehead and pulls the belt loose, letting the robe gape open down the middle.

I expect him to step back to watch it fall away, but he doesn't. He slides his large, warm hand under it, gliding against my skin at my waist, then back to cup my bare ass.

He takes a sharp breath and whispers, "You're naked."

"Yeah."

"Are you always naked when you sleep?"

"Unless I just fall down in my clothes, yes."

"I didn't bring condoms," he says, disappointment hanging heavy in his voice.

"I do this stuff for a living," I remind him with a grin. "I've got pregnancy covered, and I'm as clean as a person gets."

His lips twitch. "Me, too." He kisses my forehead again, then my cheek, and he's pushing my robe off my shoulders to pool around my feet. He lays his lips over mine, not moving them, just resting as his hands move from my shoulders to my breasts. Rather than grope, his fingers lightly skim my nipples, making them pucker in readiness, wanting his lips.

But his lips are still on mine, and now they begin to move. Slowly, lazily, fitting the mood perfectly, his soft lips brush over mine, back and forth. He nibbles the corner, making my skin break out in goosebumps.

He guides me onto the bed, but before he can settle in, I pull at the hem of his T-shirt, tucked into his jeans.

"You're way over dressed."

He smiles against my mouth, and then he's gone to quickly discard his clothes. He went from lazy and slow to The Flash in 2.1 seconds, and now he's standing next to me, all six-foot-five-ish of him, tanned and muscular and *hard*.

Hard everywhere.

"You can come back here now."

He smiles and covers my body with his, but rather than kiss me all over, he braces himself on his elbows on either side of my head and holds my gaze in his.

"Hannah."

"Yeah."

"You're sexier than I ever imagined, and I can't wait to sink inside you."

I can only smile at him.

"But if you think you're running this show, you're sorely mistaken, sweetheart."

His lips are on mine again and his hands are buried in my hair, and I'm already lost to him. To his hands and body and mouth, and he's only just started.

He kisses my jawline to my ear, then down my neck to my collarbone. My legs are restless, scissoring in anticipation, as he pulls one nipple into his mouth and tugs gently, then harder. He's worrying the other with his fingers, and it's like there's a line directly to my pussy, making it pulse with every tug of his lips.

My fingers are in his hair, fisted, holding on for dear life. Jesus, I'm ready to come and he hasn't even touched me farther south than my tits.

How am I going to survive this?

But then he drags his nose down my tummy, over my navel, and spreads my legs wide, and all rational thought flies right out the window.

Holy hell on wheels.

My wish from earlier is being granted as his mouth travels over me. My thighs, biting and licking his way up to the crease where my leg meets my core. He brushes his nose over my clit, then goes to work on the other thigh, making me writhe and curse, fisting the sheets.

"Do you have something to say?" he asks and looks up at me with blazing green eyes.

"You're killing me," I grind out through gritted teeth.

"You don't like this?" He bites my tender inner thigh gently and makes me moan in pleasure. "Are you sure, because it sounds like you like it."

"Dear God, I like it."

"What about this?" His fingers stroke my outer labia, just enough to spread the wetness around, and make me about come out of my skin. "Do you like this?"

"Oh yeah."

He chuckles and reaches up to cup my breast, flicking his thumb over the nipple. "Your breasts are perfect."

"Small."

"Perfect," he says again, and with his hand still covering said breast, he holds my gaze as he lowers his mouth to my core, sucking my clit between his lips, and my whole world shatters around me, sending me into another dimension. My head falls back, and all I can do is arch my back and moan as he makes me feel things that I didn't even know were possible.

Like shivers and contractions and my legs shaking uncontrollably.

He's a wizard. This is fucking wizardry.

He moves his mouth off my clit and down to my lips, licking and nibbling, and the next thing I know, he pushes two fingers inside me as he moves back up my body, covering me fully.

"Look at me."

I open my eyes to find his face hovering over mine.

"I'm going to see this happen this time." His fingers are moving, twisting, inside me, brushing against a spot that's making every hair on my body tingle.

I bite my lip and close my eyes, but his voice is firm. "Open."

I comply, and he presses the flat of his hand against my clit, and I fall apart, crying out as he watches me in maybe the most intimate moment of my life.

Before I float all the way back down to earth, Brad moves between my legs, pushing my knees up, and presses his cock against my sopping wet core.

"You're sure?"

"Please, God, don't stop now."

That's all he needs to hear. He sinks inside me, balls deep, and rests there, breathing hard and watching me closely.

"You're so fucking tight," he growls. He falls to his elbows and buries his face in my neck, kissing me there as his hips rear back and then push against me again, picking up a pace that's steady and sure, but not hard or too fast.

I feel so full. On fire. And when he lifts his head

and smiles down at me, I feel adored. As weird as it sounds, that's exactly the way I feel right now.

Like he just can't get enough of me.

He holds my gaze as he moves a bit faster, pushing just a little harder, and finally succumbs to his own release.

"Holy shit," he whispers, trying to catch his breath.

"Yeah," I agree and drag my fingers down his face. "Holy shit."

"Can't you call in sick today?" Brad asks me about two hours later after we've cleaned ourselves up, then got messy again before eating some eggs and bacon.

Sexy mornings should happen more often. They're highly underrated.

"I don't think so," I reply and bite my lip in disappointment. "But we have two more hours before I have to be there. Don't you have to go into work?"

"I should," he says with a sigh. "After yesterday, I'll have some paperwork to see to, and I need to get reports from everyone regarding the electricity in the water."

"Are people able to swim and boat yet?"

"Yeah, I lifted that ban late last night when I got a call saying all power that runs under the lake has been shut off for now while they figure out what the fuck went wrong." He sighs and rubs his hand over his face, and I'm sorry that I asked. He was finally relaxed.

"I'm sorry," I say and straddle his lap. We're on the couch, lounging with Sadie now curled up on my recliner. I cup his face in my hands and kiss him sweetly. "You're not supposed to be thinking about that right now."

He cups my ass, gripping firmly, and smiles up at me. "What should I think about?"

"Well, there was some pretty impressive sexy time this morning."

"We could keep that trend going," he suggests as I unzip his pants and set him free, already hard again. I'm in a sundress, with no panties, so it's easy to slide right over him, making us both sigh in lust.

"God, you're fucking amazing," he says, pulling my dress up over my head so he can get his hands on my breasts. "Beautiful."

"You feel *so good.*" I'm moving faster, riding him and glorying in how he feels from this angle. "So deep."

"God, babe." He takes my nipple into his mouth, and I can't help it. I fall apart at the seams, bearing down on him so hard that he has no choice but to come with me. I collapse against him, breathing hard.

"Hannah. You asked me before what helps, remember?"

"I do."

"It's you." He cups my face and kisses me softly. "It's just you."

"Is it weird that the hospital has better food than some of the restaurants in town?" I ask Drake the next afternoon. I've been running back and forth between the clinic and the hospital all day because I have a patient carrying twins who went into labor this morning. She's still in labor, six hours later, but there's no distress and she's laboring well. Now that my appointments are finished for the day, I can hang out here at the hospital to be close by, just in case.

So, I'm having a quick late lunch with Drake while my patient takes a break, catching a quick nap.

"I've been in a few hospitals with good food," he says and sprinkles pepper over his avocado salad.

"I guess I always expect it to suck." I shrug and watch my friend, who has a frown on his handsome face. "So what's been going on with you? Are you dating anyone?"

"Hell no," he replies and licks a drop of lemon dressing off his thumb. "Women are trouble."

"How so?"

"They start to get clingy and hint that they want a ring on their finger. And by *hint* I mean state it under no uncertain terms, and by ring I mean a six-ty-thousand-dollar rock.

"Like I said, women are trouble."

"True story," I reply with a nod, and then giggle.

Drake sits back and watches me closely. "You're dating someone."

"True story," I repeat and take a big bite of a chicken tender so I don't have to answer his next question right away.

"Who?"

"Bffd mmm."

He raises a brow and waits for me to swallow my food.

"Try that again."

"Brad Hull."

"The police chief?"

"Do you know of another one?"

He looks genuinely surprised. "I actually like Brad."

"Did you think I'd decide to date someone you don't like?"

"I'm surprised you're dating at all. You're usually too much of a workaholic like me."

"I'm still a workaholic, but so is he." I shrug. "So we only see each other a couple of times during the week, but it's nice to find a guy who understands the long hours, you know? Who doesn't complain about it. I mean, he did ask if I could call in sick yesterday, but that's just because the sexy time was off the charts."

"TMI," he says and takes a bite of his salad. "Is he nice to you?"

"Yes, he plays nice." I roll my eyes. "Plus, Sadie is such a sweetie."

"This is a threesome situation?" he asks, blinking rapidly.

"What are you, twelve?"

"On a scale of one to ten, yes." He grins. "Who's Sadie?"

"His dog."

"You've fallen for a guy's dog?"

"She's a super sweet dog," I reply defensively. "She's a retired police dog."

"You know, you could just adopt your own dog. You don't need a man for that."

"Ha ha." I throw a french fry at him and then laugh. "I like both him and the dog. He knows about the anxiety, and he's actually really understanding."

"Wow," Drake says with surprise. "You're serious about this one."

"He gets me," I reply. "So yeah, I want to see where this goes."

"Good for you, Han. Maybe we'll go on a double date sometime."

"I thought you said you're not dating anyone?"

He raises a brow again, and I dissolve into laughter. "Okay, I get it. Sure, we can do that."

My phone rings. "This is Dr. Malone."

"This is Siobhan," my nurse says. "Your patient wants to see you."

"I'm on my way."

I hang up and sigh. "Lunch is over for me. I'm being summoned."

"Take it with you."

"Oh, I am. I'll hide in my office and eat the rest later." I wink at him and turn, but he calls me back. "Yeah?"

"You look happy. I like it."

"Thanks." I smile and hurry away, wondering what's up with the patient. She might just be nervous and need another pep talk. That happens all the time, and is perfectly normal.

I stow my half eaten lunch in my office, wipe my mouth off, grab my stethoscope and hurry into the patient's room.

"What's happening in here?"

"Something's wrong," Jennifer, my patient says. Her husband is holding her hand and looks at me with desperation in his eyes.

I immediately look at the monitors, and everything looks normal.

"There are no warning signs here," I reply, but

I lay my hand on her belly, and she writhes in pain.

"It feels like my whole body is being squeezed by a giant hand."

"Well, you're having a baby. You're having *two* babies, and it's going to hurt. Did you go to birthing classes?"

"We did," Trent says with a nod.

"Great. Remember your breathing."

"Right." Jennifer nods. "Breathing." She begins to breathe quickly, pursing her lips and staring at Trent in concentration. The fetal monitor begins to move up, indicating another one, and she squeezes his hand even harder, making him wince.

"See?" I get her attention, pointing to the monitor. "You can see here when a contraction is coming, when it peaks, and when it's coming back down. If it helps, watch this and breathe with it. I'm going to check you real quick."

I turn away and wash my hands, then reach for the gloves. Jennifer is still breathing, and I expect to find that she might be already dilated to about an eight, if she's in this much pain already.

I take a deep breath, telling my brain to shut off. I've delivered hundreds of babies, and I wouldn't do this for all of the money in the world. No way. I'm not going to turn my body inside out like this.

Nope.

But I put a smile on my face, and urge her to spread her legs so I can reach in to see how ready her body is to give birth to these babies.

Two centimeters.

That's it?

I pull away and throw the gloves away, then wash my hands again.

"Well?" she asks. "Something's wrong, isn't it?"

"Not at all," I reassure her. "Jennifer, you're dilated at two centimeters."

"Only two?" Trent asks, reading my mind.

"I'm afraid so. I know you're uncomfortable, and if you want to elect for a cesarean section, we can still do that."

"No, I want to have them naturally," she insists.

"Are you sure you don't even want some medication?" I ask. "There are two babies here, Jennifer."

"No meds." She shakes her head and I sigh. She's at a two, which tells me she has many hours ahead of her to labor, and she doesn't want the drugs.

Take the drugs!

Always take the drugs. I know, many people would frown at that philosophy, but I've seen a lot of natural births. I'm *never* birthing anything, but if I did, I'd take all of the drugs.

"Okay, that's your choice," I reply, calm as can be. "I recommend getting up and walking around a bit. Up and down the hallway. That sometimes helps. After you've done that for a while, we'll put you in the bathtub. A nice bath will sometimes help your muscles relax."

"Let's do that now," she says, but I shake my head.

"There's no speedy way to do this," I reply. "Babies come when they're ready. I think we're going to be here most of the night, but you might surprise me. Let's get you up walking, and we'll go from there."

She nods and gestures for her husband to pass her the pink terrycloth bathrobe over the reclining chair.

She also brought bunny slippers.

"I like your hospital style," I say with a smile.

"I figured I should be comfortable. Well, my feet anyway."

"Absolutely. Oh, and have Trent massage your feet, too. That will help you relax."

"What helps me relax?" Trent asks.

"You're not pushing two babies out today, my friend. It's all about helping Jennifer relax."

He sighs, but smiles at his wife. "We've got this."

Jennifer doubles over in pain and starts to breathe, leaning on Trent's arms.

Yeah, no. No babies for me.

CHAPTER SEVEN

Hannah

"THANK YOU," JENNIFER SAYS twenty-three hours later through tear-filled eyes. "Thank you for staying with me all night."

"I wasn't going anywhere," I assure her and smile down at one of the babies in her arms. "I'm sorry we had to deliver them by cesarean after all."

She shrugs and smiles at her daughter. "They're here, and they're safe, and that's all that really matters."

"My colleague is here now, and I'm going to do a few things to finish up and head home. I want you to rest today. I know your family will be excited to be here, but I want you to limit visitors today. I'll give instructions to your nurse. Let her be the bad guy, Jenn. All of you need rest, and I mean it."

She nods. "I know. I'm pretty tired."

That makes two of us. I close my laptop and walk out the door to the nurse's station.

I'm still in my scrubs. I'm so damn exhausted I'm surprised I'm still walking. I want to curl up somewhere soft and warm and sleep for about four days.

Maybe five days.

I'm going to finish up my notes and go home. I'm not going to talk to anyone because I'll get stuck here for longer. Do *not* make eye contact with anyone at the nurse's station. Just keep walking to the office.

But when I approach the nurse's station, everyone is grinning at me, sipping coffee and munching on bagels.

And my stomach immediately growls.

"If you tell me none of that is left, I might throw a temper tantrum here and now."

Lucy, a nurse that I've worked with since I moved here, grins and passes me a coffee and a note.

"This was delivered," she says with a wink. "All of this is for you, but it's for all of us, too."

"You're speaking in riddles," I reply, my exhausted brain not able to keep up. So I open the note and feel everything in me soften.

Hannah,

You have to be exhausted and running on empty. Here is some fuel. Call me later.

Brad

"He brought me coffee from *Sips* and bagels from *Little Deli*."

"And thank the good lord for it," Lucy replies. "Because he brought enough for everyone."

"And then some," another nurse, Betty, says.

"He was here?" I ask.

"No, Mrs. Blakely delivered them."

"I've always liked Mrs. Blakely," I murmur, speaking of the owner of *Little Deli*. "And he got my usual coffee."

"You should call and thank him," Lucy says.

"Do you guys even know who *he* is?" I ask.

"Honey, this is a small town. We've all known for a few days now that you've been dating Chief Hull." Betty takes a sip of her coffee. "And I'd like to say, you should keep dating him if he's going to bring us treats."

I shake my head and laugh, walking toward my office. I need to call and thank him.

"Hull," he says into his phone, sounding distracted.

"I'd like to report a disturbance at the hospital amongst the nurses over a bagel delivery," I say and smile when he chuckles in my ear. "Thank you, Brad."

"You're welcome. I figured you'd need something."

"I do." *I could use you.* "I'm almost wrapped up here, and then I'm going to go home and sleep, then wake up and eat another bagel for dinner."

"Don't eat a bagel for dinner, sweetheart. I'll bring something."

I rub my chest, just over my heart and the slight ache I have there whenever he speaks to me in this soft voice.

"I'll be so out of it, it won't matter."

"If it doesn't matter, then I'm coming over," he says and I just smile, already excited to see him.

"Okay. There's a key under the flowerpot in the corner of the porch. Just let yourself in because I probably won't hear the doorbell."

"Are you okay to drive home?"

"Yeah, it's not far." I yawn and then take a sip of my delicious java. "And I have coffee to sustain me until I get there. Thanks to a handsome police officer I know."

"Who is he? I'll kill him."

I snort. "You're no killer."

"This has turned into an odd conversation." He pulls the phone away from his face to talk to someone in the room with him and then comes back. "Sorry, Hannah, I have to go. Be careful getting home and I'll see you later."

"Thank you for all of this. Sincerely."

"You're welcome."

And with that he's gone and I'm left sitting in my office, barely able to keep my eyes open, despite the caffeine kick.

I need to go crash.

After quickly finishing up a few last notes, I gather a few bagels, a tub of cream cheese, and my personal things and then head toward home.

When I pull into my driveway, someone pulls in right behind me.

"Hey," Grace says when I get out of my car. "I saw you drive past me at the four-way stop a few blocks back, and thought I'd stop by for a second. How are you?"

"Exhausted." I lead her up my porch and into my house. "I haven't been home since yesterday morning."

"That's a long shift," she says and peers inside the bagel bag. "Are you willing to share one of these bagels from Mrs. Blakely?"

"Sure. Let's do it. I'm starving."

I reach for a knife to spread the cream cheese. "What are you up to today?"

"Well, that's the other reason I came by. Jacob and I are leaving later today for New York. I guess he has a couple of meetings, and a swanky party to go to. I have a dress and shoes, but I don't have a pretty clutch, and I know you have that Gucci one that Drake got you for Christmas a few years back."

"Never been used," I confirm. "You're welcome to borrow it."

"Thanks." She grins and takes a bite of her bagel. "How are things with you and Brad?"

I smile, the thought of Brad waking me right up. "Really good." I nod. "Like, really, *really* good. He's such a good guy. He's sweet and strong. He cares deeply about his friends. His dog is the *best*."

I take a sip of my now almost cold coffee, thinking of him. "He's a gentleman. And I mean he's a *gentle man.* Sometimes they're not the same thing."

"Agreed."

"I don't think I've ever met anyone like him. The sex? Holy shit, Grace."

"Wow," she says, watching me avidly. "That good?"

"I didn't even know some of the things he's done to me were possible, and I'm no virgin."

"Atta girl," she says, holding her fist out for a bump. "I don't care what anyone says, sexual chemistry is super important."

"Absolutely. And he also likes to hold me. He's always touching me. And he recently told me that the only thing in the world that calms him down is me."

"Jesus, Hannah, you're in love!"

I stop and stare at her, blinking rapidly.

"Well, no."

"I've only ever talked this way about the man I love," she says reasonably. "And I think it's fantastic. I'm so excited for you."

"Wait." I stand and pace the kitchen, thinking about this. "Maybe this is too good to be true. I mean, I haven't really known him that long."

"Only a few years," Grace says with a smirk.

"I mean *really* known him. What if he's not at all what I think he is? What if he's an alcoholic?"

"He's not your dad," she reminds me and I shake the thought off.

"You're right. Besides, I don't think he could function at his job as well as he does if he was drunk all the time."

"Definitely not."

"But what if he's secretly a serial killer? Or has other wives? Am I going to be a sister wife?"

"I haven't heard any talk about *any* wives, and I don't see a ring on your finger, so I'm going to say no."

"He could have kids. I've never asked him if he has kids."

"No kids," she says and tilts her head to the side. "What are you trying to do here?"

"There has to be another shoe that's going to drop," I reply and sit across from her. "Everything is too perfect. *He's* too perfect."

"Is he really perfect? Does he never have bad breath? Maybe he leaves his socks on the floor? Certainly he must fart."

I smirk. "I've never stayed at his house, so I don't know if he leaves his socks on the floor. He's a human being, so I'm sure there are faults in there somewhere that I just haven't found yet."

"Right, because you're still discovering each other. This is the best part of the relationship, when all of the butterflies happen and you can't stay away from each other. It's exciting."

"Are you saying you don't feel this anymore with Jacob?"

"Hell no, the man still gives me butterflies after a year of marriage," she says with a smile. "And, would it be weird if I'm your patient?"

"Why?"

She just sits there and smiles, and I feel like I'm missing something. Finally, she rolls her eyes and points to her stomach, and I feel my eyes widen in surprise.

"Oh my God! Really? You're pregnant?"

"That's what the stick said," she replies and pats her belly. "But we're not talking about me. We're talking about you and the perfect Brad."

"He's probably flawed," I say and frown. "Maybe."

"It sounds like you're deciding whether to stay with him, or run."

"Why would I run? I don't want to run."

"Good, because that would be really stupid. So maybe you're just, I don't know. What are you?"

"I'm dumb."

"No, you're not," she says with a giggle.

"I can't describe how I feel. It sounds weird to my own ears, but it's like I already know him. It's a connection that I can't explain, and when I'm with him, I feel so calm. It's scary."

"If it wasn't scary, it wouldn't be real," she says with a shrug, and I narrow my eyes at her.

"You're smart."

"I know."

"And if you think anyone but me is delivering that baby, you're on crack."

She laughs and reaches out to squeeze my hand. "Good. Because I don't like strangers looking at my hooha."

"It's a vagina."

"Hooha."

"Repeat after me." I grab her face in my hands. "Va-gi-na."

"Hoo-ha."

We dissolve in giggles and then I take a deep breath and push my hair over my shoulder. "I'm glad you came by. Since we don't live together anymore, I miss you."

"I miss you, too. Did I mention that we're having a big party at the lake house for the fourth of July?"

"That's a month away."

"But do you work?"

I check my calendar, and smile with excitement. "I don't! So unless someone has a baby, I'll be there."

"Cool." Grace smiles. "I've invited Jenna and Max too, so bring Brad with you."

"Yes, ma'am. Who else is coming?"

"Not anyone else I can think of. It's going to be on the smaller side. I invited the King family, but they have their own traditions for the holiday. We'll go out on the lake and eat a ton of food and we have a great view of the fireworks from our deck."

"Sounds like fun."

She checks her phone when it pings. "This is Jacob. I'd better go."

"Oh, I'll grab the clutch for you."

I hurry back to my closet and pull the small handbag out of its protective covering and take it out to my friend. "Have tons of fun, and send me photos."

"I will." She hugs me tightly. "And stop stressing out about this Brad thing. Just enjoy the super hot sex and being with someone nice to you. One day at a time."

I nod and then hide my smile behind my hand when she runs into the doorframe.

My sweet Grace is anything but graceful.

She rubs her shoulder where I'm sure she'll get a bruise, and waves from the car.

I should go crash, but now that I've talked about Brad and finished my coffee, I'm surprisingly not sleepy. Exhausted to the bone, but not sleepy.

Damn it.

I glance around my small house, wondering if there's something to clean, but my housekeeper was here yesterday and it's all done.

I can't exercise. It might kill me.

I could read, except my eyes are tired.

Why won't my brain shut off?

"I need a pet," I mutter. "Something to talk to and snuggle up to when Brad's not available."

And then an idea forms in my head. I reach for my phone and dial Brad's number.

"You're awake," he says with surprise.

"I am and I'm wondering if I can borrow your dog."

There's a pause. "Is everything okay?"

"Yeah, I just want some company and all of you normal people are at work. So can I please borrow Sadie?"

"Sure, she's here at my office. I can bring her to you."

"I'll come get her. It's not far."

"You're sure?"

"Yes. See you in a few."

Excited at the idea of seeing not only Sadie but

her sexy as hell owner as well, I grab my keys and bag and hurry out to the car. The police station is only a five minute drive from my house.

When I pull into the parking lot, Brad is standing on the sidewalk with Sadie on her leash.

"Hey," I say when I climb out of the car and join them. "Thanks for letting me borrow her."

"I'm beginning to think you're just with me for my dog."

I'm feeling sassy, so I reach up and fist my hand in the back of his hair, pulling him down to kiss me. It's quick, but it's hot, and when he pulls away, I lick my lips.

"Well, I guess as long as we understand each other," I say and he frowns, as if he doesn't understand what I mean. "About Sadie. I'm just sticking around for her."

"Right." He passes me her leash and Sadie nudges my leg, ready to be petted.

"Do you want to go home with me, sweet girl?" She smiles up at me sweetly. "I think that means yes."

"I'll bring some food for her when I bring you dinner," he says. "She's done her business not long ago, so you're good to go."

"Great." I smile up at him and turn away, leading her to my car. I open the door and she happily jumps in, settling into the passenger seat. "She's done this before."

He laughs. "Go get some rest. I'll see you this evening."

I nod and take us both home. Sadie is excited when I open the front door for her. She runs for the couch, but I stop her.

"No, girl, we're going to bed." Her ears perk up and she turns her head to the side, listening. "Follow me."

I walk to my cool, dark bedroom, strip out of my clothes, and collapse onto the bed, pulling my big, heavy comforter over me. I have an extra heavy comforter that is supposed to help with anxiety.

So far, it works.

I also have blackout shades for the windows because I work at night so often, and I keep the AC low. I need a cold bedroom.

Once I'm settled in, I pat the bed next to me and Sadie jumps up with me, laying her head on my arm. "Thanks for hanging out with me today, sweet girl."

She whines happily, and I decide to send Brad a selfie of us. We both smile at the camera and I shoot it off to him.

Several moments later, he replies with, "Wish I was there with you."

I just send back, "Soon" and snuggle up to this sweet dog.

"Did you know you're very cuddly?" I ask her, petting her super soft head and ears. "You are. And your fur on your head is so soft. You're such a good girl."

Sadie's eyes are blinking heavily, and I can feel mine starting to get heavy too. Finally, the exhaustion is catching up with me and I can sleep for a long while.

But I can't help but continue to murmur to the dog in my arms.

"Your daddy is pretty great. I'm sure you already know that. You're quite loyal to him. I think we have that in common already. Can I tell you a secret, Sadie?"

She just snores, oblivious to the serious conversation we're having.

"I'm falling in love with him. Grace is right." I pet her belly, my mind on the man across town. "I don't know how he's stayed single all this time. And the anxiety in me wants to tear that thought apart, pondering if he has mother issues, or daddy issues, or any other issues that have sabotaged all of his relationships before me.

"But I don't think I'm going to do that this time. I trust him, Sadie, and that's big for me. I admire him. And my God, I love him."

I kiss her head and close my eyes, letting the heavy blanket and snoring Sadie lull me to sleep.

CHAPTER EIGHT

Brad

THE KEY IS WHERE she said it would be, under the planter in the corner of her porch. I should talk to her about the dangers of having a key in such an obvious place. It's not safe.

I have lasagna from Ciao in my hands, along with a bag of food for the dog, which I'll leave here.

I have a feeling Sadie will be spending a bit of time here.

And frankly, that's okay with me. She may seem like a big teddy bear, but if there's danger nearby, Sadie is a fierce protector. If I can't be here with Hannah, it makes me feel better knowing that Sadie is.

The house is quiet as I walk through. I set the pan of lasagna in the oven and set it to low to keep it warm, then go in search of my girls.

The bedroom is dark, even though it's still perfectly sunny outside. The light from the hall casts on Hannah's sweet face. Sadie immediately sees me and jumps off the bed to greet me. I kneel to pet her and kiss her head, then point for her to go to the living room, which she does without hesitation.

I step to the bed and look down at Hannah. I should leave her be. She has only been asleep for about four hours, and I know she needs more. And I will leave her alone, but first I want to feel her.

I slide into the bed with her and pull her to me. Her eyes open, and she blinks in confusion.

"Brad?"

"Yes, ma'am."

"I'm sorry, I'll wake up."

"No," I scoot onto my back and she snuggles up to me, her head resting on my chest. She wraps her slender arm around my midsection, holding on tightly. "Stay asleep, beautiful girl. I just want to hold you for a while."

She sighs and drifts immediately back to sleep. I kiss her forehead and hold her to me for a long moment. I haven't seen her in a few days, and I missed her. Her laugh, her voice, her body.

Everything.

It hasn't been long, but she's wiggled her way into my life and now I don't know what it would look like without her in it.

I don't want to know.

I can hear Sadie getting restless, so I slip out from under Hannah and smile when she snuggles up to her pillow, burying her face in it. I pad out to the kitchen and pour Sadie's dinner for her, then let her outside to do her business. While she's out in Hannah's fenced backyard, I run out to my truck and fetch my computer and cell phone.

Sadie joins me back inside, and she gives me the side eye when I won't let her lay on the couch, insisting she lay on the floor.

"Hannah is spoiling you."

She huffs in disapproval, but before long she's snoring. I turn the TV on and let a baseball game play in the background while I work for a while. There's always paperwork to do, calls to make, things to follow up on. If I'd still had Sadie with me, I would have stayed at the office well into the evening.

But this was a great excuse to leave. I can work from here just as well, and I want to be here when Hannah wakes up.

The reports from the electric company are in regarding the Reardon accident. That's exactly what it was, an accident. No foul play and no one's fault. A power line had surfaced at the bottom of the lake and Kendall paid the price.

We're lucky more weren't killed.

The funeral was yesterday, and I stood by my friend as he buried another person he loved more than anything. I can't imagine the pain of losing a child, and I hope to God I never do.

But I was honest when I told Hannah that she calms me. She clears the demons away, and brings lightness to my heavy heart that I haven't felt in a very long time.

Maybe never.

Sadie yawns and turns over on the floor, exposing her belly. I'm tired myself, my eyes heavy from hours of computer work. I close the computer, intending to just take a small break.

"Hey."

Someone is running their hands through my hair, scratching their nails against my scalp.

It feels fucking amazing.

I open one eye to find Hannah standing next to me, smile down at me. I'm surprised I didn't hear her approach. I'm a light sleeper, hearing every noise around me.

"Hi." I drag my hand down my face and frown at the time. "I must have fallen asleep."

"Looks like it."

I reach out, wrap my arm around her waist, and pull her into my lap, nuzzling her neck. "You smell so fucking good." She's citrus and a touch of something else that I can't put my finger on.

She's Hannah, and she's still touching me with those magical fingers, running them through my hair, over my face.

"I thought I dreamed you," she says and kisses my cheek. "But I'm so glad I didn't."

"You didn't. I brought dinner."

"I can smell it. That's what woke me."

"Are you hungry?"

"Starving."

I smile against her neck and then let her squirm out of my grasp. She holds her hand out to help me out of the chair, which I accept.

"I guess I should feed you if you're starving."

"Yes, you should."

Her eyes are still heavy and there are dark circles under them. She's not going to be awake for long.

"Does lasagna sound good?"

"Everything sounds good," she replies and sits in a chair at the table while I dish us both up a good-sized helping. "I would even settle for a left-over bagel at this point. Which were delicious, by the way. Is this from Ciao?"

"Yep."

"Mmm." She sniffs it when I put it in front of her, and then digs in. "I've never had this before. Oh my God, so good."

I nod in agreement, and we're both quiet as we make our way through our meal. When she's finished, I carry both of our plates to the sink, and when I turn around, I can't help but laugh.

Hannah is sitting with her chin propped in her hand, eyes closed.

"Are you sleeping?"

"No."

"You look like you're sleeping."

"Not yet. I just can't keep my eyes open. I hope I don't have narcolepsy."

"Narcawhaty?"

"Narcolepsy." She smiles. "It's that condition where you fall asleep all the time."

"I don't think you have that."

She still doesn't open her eyes. "You don't know. You're not a doctor."

"You're exhausted because you delivered a baby."

"Two. Two babies. And I can't tell you their names because of the law."

"I *am* the law, sweetheart."

"You know what I mean." She yawns, still not opening her eyes, and I can't stand it anymore. I scoop her up in my arms, and her fingers immediately dive into the hair at the back of my head, making my dick stand at attention.

It seems this woman has found my Achilles heel. And it's nowhere near my feet.

When I reach her bed and set her down, she leans in to press her lips to my ear.

"Stay," she whispers.

"Baby, you're exhausted. You need to sleep."

"I will sleep. After."

She smiles up at me and lets her robe fall away, revealing her gorgeous naked body, and it takes everything in me not to pin her down and fuck her into the mattress.

Not that I won't do that, and soon.

But not right now.

Not tonight.

"Hannah—"

"Please stay," she says again and scoots over, making room for me on the bed. "If you're not in the mood for sex, that's okay. Just stay for a while."

"I'm always in the mood for you," I reply and hastily remove my clothes. "I can't stop thinking about you, daydreaming about you."

I slip into the bed next to her and pull her against me, tipping my forehead against hers. Her hand glides up my arm, over my shoulder, and into the hair at the back of my head, and I go cross-eyed.

"Your hair is so soft here," she whispers.

"I'm glad you like it."

"Why do you have goosebumps?"

"Because you're running your fingers through my hair." I smile and kiss her lips softly. "Seems that's a thing for me."

"Interesting." She kisses my chin. "I want to find some of your other *things*."

"You're welcome to go on a scouting mission anytime."

I feel her smile against my neck, and suddenly she rolls on top of me, straddling me and rubbing her bare pussy against the length of my cock.

"Yes, that's one of the things," I say, sarcasm dripping from the words, and she laughs, then bites my nipple, not at all gently. "You have a sudden burst of energy."

"Imagine that," she replies. She has one hand planted on the bed next to my head and the other is flat against my stomach, headed south. She scoots down as well, kissing my hot skin where her hand has been, and settles between my legs, my cock gripped firmly in her hands, her tongue making circles along the ridge around the head.

"Fucking Jesus," I groan and grip onto the sheets.

"No, you're fucking Hannah," she says and then sinks down over me, sucking and licking. She's making noises, which only intensifies the heaviness in my balls and electricity moving through me.

I'm going to fucking come, and I don't want to do that yet.

"Hannah," I warn her, but she shakes her head and keeps going, gripping me hard and I have to take her by the shoulders, pull her off of me, and switch our positions, tucking her beneath me.

"I'm not going to come in your mouth," I growl

before sinking slowly inside her. "Not today."

"Another day then?" She moans and hitches her legs up around my sides, gripping my ass in her strong hands and pulling me more tightly against her.

"Maybe." She cocks a brow and I smirk. "Some women don't like that."

"I'm not some women."

"No, you're not." I drag my fingertips down her cheek and cup her neck and jaw, just able to see her eyes from the glow of the hallway. "You're fucking amazing."

"You're good for my ego."

I pull my hips back and then push in again, deeper than before and watch her eyes widen in lust and pleasure.

"I'm not feeding your damn ego. You're magnificent." I kiss her lips, nibble the corner of her mouth and then sink into her, tangling our tongues, tasting her. She's moaning against my mouth, and her fingers have tangled in my hair again, and that's it. I can't stop myself from picking up the pace, pushing harder, and cursing under my breath when she bears down and squeezes me as she comes around me.

I bury my face in her hair and follow her over; the world falls away and I'm lost in her.

There's no going back.

I'm hers.

"So, you've never been kayaking?" I ask Hannah about a week later as we drive the forty miles or so into Glacier National Park.

"No, it's always scared me. I know how to swim, but you always hear of people rolling over in their kayak, and I don't want to do that. Ever."

"Well, I have sit-on-top kayaks, and they're less likely to tip over." I smile over at her and squeeze her hand in mine, feeling the tension in her. This makes her nervous, but she's willing to give it a try, and that says a lot about her. "And if you hate it, we can just hike a bit."

"Okay." She nods and looks in the backseat at her backpack.

"You grabbed the bear spray."

"I know, I'm just checking." She fidgets. "I know it's weird to you that I have this fear, but I can't turn it off. I can't describe it, I just have it, and I can't make it go away."

"You don't have to describe it," I assure her and turn on the road that leads up to Bowman Lake, a lesser-known lake that tends to be less rull of tour-ists this time of year. "You're right, I don't under-stand it, but I have other quirks that I can't explain either."

"Like what?"

"Remember when I took you to my house that day that you hurt your ankle, and I made you stay in the truck while I checked the house?"

"Yes."

"It's habit, anxiety now that I think about it, to walk through the entire property when I get home to make sure nothing is disturbed. I lock up tight, and I have alarms and cameras, but I have to do a sweep before I can settle in."

"And you don't know why?" she asks.

I know why.

"Actually, when I was a kid, and my dad was chief, we had been out as a family around Christmas time. I don't remember where we'd been. But we came home and there was a man in our house, drunk and pissed off and he came to the chief's house to confront him about it."

"Oh my God."

"It was scary. Dad had a weapon on him, and I don't think we were ever in danger. I don't remember what the man was upset about. Maybe his wife had kicked him out for beating her, I'm not sure. But I remember that he was *so pissed off.* Dad lured him outside and Mom rushed us into a back bedroom and called for backup, which came quickly. But I don't think I'll forget walking into the house and seeing a stranger there."

"No. I wouldn't forget that either."

"I didn't check the house before," I continue. "And I don't think it ever occurred to me that that's why I do it now. As soon as I became chief, I started the routine, and now I realize that's why."

"It makes sense," she says with a nod, and then points to the red building of the small bakery in a town of only a couple hundred people. "Best pastries in the state."

"Let's stop."

The bakery is also a small convenience store for people who may need water, batteries, or other supplies. This is just a day trip, and we're prepared, so we each just choose a bear claw, check out, and get back in the truck.

"The road to the lake is bumpy and twisty," I warn her.

"Okay." She smiles and takes a bite of her pastry. "Thank the good lord for these nuggets of deliciousness. I'm gonna work the calories off on the lake."

I nod and concentrate on the road. Despite being a popular destination among locals, the road is dirt, full of potholes, and incredibly windy. About two miles up, Hannah lays her hand over her stomach.

"Maybe I shouldn't have eaten that."

"I'm sorry, I'm trying to take it easy. I can't go fast, but there's nothing I can do about the road."

"It's not your fault," she says and rolls the window down. "Are you sure we're going the right way? This looks like it's never travelled."

"It's travelled," I assure her. "But it'll never be paved. The locals like that it's not swarming with tourists."

"I like that, too," she says with a smile. "How

much longer?"

"About six miles."

"Jesus," she mutters and pushes her nose out of the window, breathing in the fresh air. "This had better be worth it."

"It is," I say and smile at her, still holding her hand. "It's stunning up here. You'll love it."

She nods and I will the road to shorten so I can get her there faster, but it's still another forty-five minutes before we arrive.

The parking lot is half full, and I find a space near the path that leads to the lake.

"There are people up here," she says with surprise.

"But not a million of them," I reply and help her out of the truck. We pull the kayaks and oars out of the truck, along with our backpacks, and I lock it up, then turn to her. "If you don't want to haul one of these down there, I'll have you stay here with one of them and I'll take one, then come back."

"Oh please." She rolls her eyes, hitches her backpack on her shoulders and reaches for her kayak and oar, then sets off to the trail. "I work out for this, remember?"

I'm going to marry her. Today.

"Impressive," I say behind her and hear her smirk.

"I'm just carrying a kayak."

"Like a badass," I reply. The lake shore is only about thirty yards away, and when we reach the water, she sets the kayak down beside her and just stares at the mountains, the glassy water, and then looks up at me with tears in her eyes. "What's wrong, sweetheart?"

"It's *so* beautiful." She shakes her head and looks around once more, her hands on her hips. "I get to live here."

"Well, close to here." I kiss her cheek and get busy showing her how to maneuver the kayak. "What do you think?"

"I think it looks easier than it is," she says with a laugh. "But I'm going to give it the old college try."

"Good girl."

I help her onto the water craft, get her settled, and watch her paddle away as if she's been doing this for years.

I quickly get my gear ready and paddle behind her, enjoying the way she's smiling and looking around her. I catch up to her and grin over at her.

"What do you think?"

"I think I need to do this more often," she says. "Are there fish in here?"

"Some," I reply. "A few salmon, trout. We might see some eagles snacking today. But this is glacier water and snow run off, so it's really too cold and sterile for there to be a lot of fish."

"You know a lot about this," she says.

"I used to volunteer up here in the summers. I thought I wanted to be a park ranger when I grew up."

"And here you are, protecting people rather than wildlife."

"Yes, ma'am." I rest my oar across my body and take a drink of water. "But I still love it here, more than almost anywhere."

"I can understand why. This lake goes on forever."

"About seven miles," I reply with a nod. "And it's a mile wide in some places. I love that the mountains change as we move down the lake."

"It's stunning, really. I know there's so much of the park that I haven't seen yet, but it always surprises me."

We paddle in silence for a while, enjoying the quiet and the beautiful day. I glance to my right and see a grizzly lazily eating berries on the shoreline, and keep it to myself. I don't want to scare her.

"I see it," she says without even looking my way.

"See what?"

"The bear. And I know they can swim. And my heart is probably going to seize, but I'm okay."

"Are you sure?"

"Yes. I'm in their house, so I have to deal with the fact that I'm going to see them. But I'm glad he's way over there, and that he's more interested in berries than me."

"She," I reply.

"She?"

I point to the two cubs playing on the rocky beach and Hannah smiles.

"They're adorable. And far away."

I nod, proud of her for putting on a brave face. I can see her hands shaking, but she doesn't immediately turn around or freak out. She's breathing deeply, and keeping an eye on the wildlife on shore.

"How many bears do you think are in this park?" she asks.

"I don't think we should talk numbers. I don't want to freak you out."

"Facts calm me," she says and raises a brow at me. "How many do you think?"

"Three hundred, give or take," I reply and watch her swallow hard. "But that's over more than a million acres, Hannah. *A million.* The odds of having an encounter that's anything other than what we just had are *so slim.*"

"I know." She shrugs one shoulder. "Like I said, I can't change it. She was beautiful, and her babies are adorable. I'm glad I saw her from a safe distance. And I don't care if I never see another one."

"You're brave."

She snorts and rests her oar on the kayak. "I'm not brave, Brad. But I'm enjoying this kayak ride. I'm so glad you brought me."

"Me too. Are you ready to turn back?"

"Is that the other head of the lake?" she asks, pointing ahead of us.

"Yes."

"Well, then I guess we should turn back, since there's nowhere else to go."

I show her how to turn around, and she's mimicking my movements. But then a bee flies by her face, and she shakes her head, flailing with her hand, and rocks the kayak too hard to recover.

She falls into the water with a shriek, and before I can jump in and help her, she's grabbed the side of the kayak and pulled herself out of the water, panting and laughing at the same time. She's soaked through.

"Are you okay?" I've paddled over to her and am holding her kayak to mine. She's started to laugh.

"Good God, that's fucking cold!" Her nipples are pressed against her soaked tank top, and she's shivering a bit, wringing her hair out. "No wonder fish don't live there. *Nothing* could live there."

"You'll warm up quickly. It's ninety today. Probably eighty on the lake."

"Whew, I'm awake now," she says and laughs again, turning her face to the sun, soaking in the warmth. "Beginner's luck."

"You're stunning."

"I'm a mess." She turns that smile to me. "If I lean your way, can you kiss me without dumping us both back in this water?"

I don't answer, I just lean toward her slowly and she follows, kissing me with not a little heat. Her lips are cold. She backs away and then her eyes widen in fear.

"Fuck! I lost the oar!"

"I saved it," I assure her and pass it to her.

"You're my hero."

I laugh and tuck her wet hair behind her ear. "Are you ready to go back?"

"Yes. I have to paddle to get my body heat back up."

"I should have brought a sweatshirt or something, just in case."

"I don't think we have the cargo space for that," she says. "I'm fine. I might just paddle faster this time."

CHAPTER NINE

Hannah

I'M NOT GOING IN that water. Not today, not ever.

I stare down into the lake, not even hearing the voices around me. It's the Fourth of July, just three weeks after being on a different lake with Brad up in the park. But this is different. This lake killed a young boy this summer, and I will *not* touch the water.

We all gathered at Jacob and Grace's house on the lake a few hours ago. And by *we all*, I mean Brad and me, Jenna, Max, along with Grace and Jacob of course.

And let's not forget Brad's *parents*.

They just arrived in town for the remainder of the summer, and I'm meeting them for the first time today, on a pontoon boat.

On killer water.

"I've heard a lot about you," Mary Hull says with a smile and takes a sip of her cold can of Coke. "I'm so happy that we get to spend the day with you."

I nod and force a smile, trying desperately to calm down. But some of our group is on a ski boat, tubing and water skiing, *in the water*, and I just can't breathe.

I'm terrified.

Not that I'll let anyone else here know that.

"Hannah?" Grace asks, frowning.

"I'm sorry, what?"

"I asked you what kind of medicine you practice, dear," Mary says. "Are you okay?"

"I'm fine." I clear my throat and try to focus, ignoring the fact that Brad is currently water skiing in the water. "I'm sorry, my mind wandered. I am an OB/GYN. I share a practice here in town."

"How lovely," Mary says with a smile. "It must be wonderful to deliver babies into the world."

"It's hard work, and sometimes sad, but I wouldn't change it for the world."

"The guys are having fun," Grace says, pointing to the boat whizzing by about a hundred yards away. Max is in the water now, with Brad, Jacob, Jenna, and Bruce, Brad's dad, in the boat. "I can't water ski. I'd drown."

"No, you wouldn't," Mary says with a laugh.

"Oh, I would," Grace assures her. "I'm as clumsy as they come. My name is not appropriate for me."

We all laugh and I finally start to relax. I decide to go up to the roof of the pontoon boat so I can sit in the sun for a little bit and just be calm.

Just *be*.

"If you ladies will excuse me, I'm going to soak in some sun."

"Won't you burn?" Mary asks.

"I'm the only redhead I know who tans," I reply with a shrug. "But I won't stay out for long."

They both nod happily and I can hear them chatting away as I climb the ladder to the top of the boat. This is an impressive watercraft. With two levels, a slide off the back, and seating for twenty, it's huge. Even this upper deck has an umbrella I can open for shade if I get too hot.

I could live on this boat.

And the best part is, there's no chance of falling into the water the way I did when we went kayaking. That was humiliating, but we laughed it off and had a great day.

I don't want there to be *any* chance that I could fall into this water. I know that Brad made sure the electrical issue was fixed, but it still happened. Someone died.

I don't want to chance it.

You're being unreasonable. And I know that. It's the anxiety. The rational side of me knows that there's nothing to be afraid of. The irrational anxious side of me doesn't give even one shit.

I'm going to over think it anyway.

I can't watch the other boat without my stomach dropping, so I turn my lounge chair in the opposite direction and sit back, breathing deeply. I'm in a bathing suit with a cover up, but I'm not too hot. It's always about ten degrees cooler on the lake. The chair is soft and plush, and before long my anxiety has calmed down and I could easily drift to sleep.

But I don't. I'm watching the shoreline off in the distance, floating by lazily. We took the boat out in the middle of the lake, directly in front of Grace and Jacob's house. From way out here, their house still looks massive. It's just been the two of them in that big house, but soon there will be three.

I'm happy for her.

"You're up here by yourself," Jenna says and sits next to me, surprising me.

"I thought you were on the other boat?"

"I had the guys bring me back here. There was a lot of testosterone on that boat." She laughs and passes me a fresh Coke. "We could go in Grace's house and make iced coffees."

"How did you just read my mind?"

"Friend, your mind is always on coffee."

"True. Maybe in a bit, the sun is so nice right now."

Jenna is in a turquoise bikini, showing off her curves. Her natural platinum blonde hair is tucked up in a sun hat, and she's wearing huge sunglasses.

"You look like a starlet today."

She smirks. "Sure."

"You look like a starlet every day. You must hear that a lot."

She shrugs one shoulder and then links her fingers over her flat belly. "Maybe I shouldn't dress nice in front of my crew."

"What do you mean?"

"You know I'm building the tree houses on the mountain, right?"

"Yes, and I'm *dying* to see them."

"I'm so irritated. My brothers are co-owners with me, but *I'm* the brains behind the operation. They're my vision, my heart, my project."

"Gotcha."

"But I guarantee you, every single day when I go to the job site and speak with someone, they either dismiss me altogether, or tell me to have my *husband* come talk to them."

"What the fuck?"

"Right?" She pats my arm and nods. "When I explain that they'll have to talk to *me*, they shake their heads and look frustrated. It pisses me off."

"It would piss me off too."

"So I've told Max and Brad to stop coming to meetings. They're all going to learn to deal with me and me *only*. I've been in real estate for over ten years. I've run my own vacation rentals, including a super fancy B&B, for almost that long. I know what I want, and I have the money to get it.

"But now they've decided to go over budget already and we're only half way built."

"Not acceptable."

"No," she agrees. "So I just fired my contractor yesterday, and now I have to find someone new. I would just do it myself, but it's three buildings, thirty feet off the ground. It's not a normal house."

"It sounds incredible."

"It will be," she says with a smile. "I can't wait for you to see them. I also have my eye on a piece of property in the park that just went on the market."

"As in, *inside* Glacier Park?"

"Yeah," she says with a nod. "There are about a dozen private residences inside the park. This one is on Lake McDonald, and it's gorgeous. I know I could rent it out most of the year."

"Absolutely. You should do it!"

"I'm sinking a shit ton of money into the tree houses right now," she says and wrinkles her nose. "But I may never have the chance to own property in the park again."

"Exactly. Do it. I'm serious. I'll go in on it with you."

"You're a good friend." A slow smile slides over her perfect lips. Jenna looks annoyingly like

Grace Kelly. If she wasn't so wonderful, we might all hate her. "I'll just get another loan for it. I *know* it would pay for itself in less than three years."

"Sounds like a no brainer."

She claps her hands excitedly. "Now to get those tree houses finished and rented out so they can start paying for themselves, too."

"Do you mind if I fold out the awning?"

"Not at all," she says as I stand and roll out the awning, casting us in blessed shade.

"That's better. I was starting to sweat, and no one wants that."

"No," Jenna says with a laugh. "My mom likes you."

"I feel bad because I was nervous and I've hardly said three words to her."

"She likes you," she says again. "And I *know* my brother likes you."

"I should hope so. He's naked with me a lot."

"Ew," Jenna says and then laughs. "But good for you guys."

"Am I missing good stuff up here?" Grace asks and joins us. "Also, side note, be *very* proud of me for climbing that ladder and not dying."

"Very proud." I smile as Grace sits opposite of us, so she can see us and takes her sunglasses off.

"I don't know how I'll get down. Me going down a ladder doesn't sound like a good idea."

"You can slide down the slide," Jenna suggests, and just like that my anxiety is in high gear again.

"I'll help you down the ladder," I offer immediately.

Grace just laughs, oblivious to my inner turmoil and changes the subject.

"Did you hear that Louise Summers sold her clothing boutique in town?"

"I did," Jenna says with a nod. "Didn't she retire?"

"Yes, and Willa Monroe bought it. She's doing some remodeling, and I saw her in the grocery store last week, and she said she's going to update it, make it super pretty and trendy. Bring in some higher end clothing lines. I'm excited to see what she does."

"I always liked Willa," Jenna says with a smile.

"Who is Willa?" I ask.

"Willa and Max used to date in high school," Jenna replies and shakes her head. "My stupid brother let her get away. She's widowed now, with a little boy, Jack."

"He's adorable," Grace says. "Has Max seen her since he's been home?"

"I doubt it," Jenna replies and looks around to make sure her brother isn't in ear shot. "I told him to call her, but he's a stubborn ass."

"Well, she's having a fun grand opening party next Friday evening, and I think we should go."

"That sounds fun," I reply. "I'm in."

"Me too," Jenna adds. "Cunningham Falls can use a trendy new clothes store. Let's plan a night of it."

"Are you guys up there?" Jacob calls out from the lower deck.

"We are," Grace calls back.

"We have food down here. I'll come get you, love."

Before Grace can reply, he's scaled up the ladder and scoops her up in his arms, kissing her sweetly.

"How are you?" he asks.

"I'm just fine. I wasn't going to try to go down the ladder without you."

"Good girl." He nuzzles her neck, then walks to the ladder and sets her down, wedging her between him and ladder, helping her down.

"He's sweet," Jenna says. "And hello, British accent."

"I know, it ups the hot factor," I reply with a laugh. "Let's go eat. I'm hungry."

We shimmy down the ladder to find everyone back on the pontoon.

"There you are," Brad says and pulls me to him for a kiss that makes my toes curl. "You look beautiful in this suit."

"Thank you. What is there to eat?"

"Sandwiches, salads, and cookies for dessert. Oh, and some fruit."

Max and Brad give each other a hard time about their water skiing adventure, Jenna, Jacob, and Grace are chatting in a corner, and Mary and Bruce are eating, watching us all with content faces.

"Are you happy to be home?" I ask them.

"Always," Bruce says with a wink. "We hardly left for thirty years because I always worked so damn much. It's been good to see some of the world with my bride."

I smile, watching how sweet Brad's parents are with each other. What must it have been like to grow up in a house that was functional?

I glance at Brad and Max, both still shirtless and in their drying swim trunks, chatting and laughing while eating their sandwiches. It's clear they all get along well, that they care for each other. The wealth that Max has come into in the past few years hasn't changed his dynamic with his family.

And let's be honest, the two Hull boys standing shirtless together is a sight to behold.

"What are you thinking over there?" Brad asks, pulling me out of my own head.

"I'm just sitting here," I reply and grin when he takes my hand and pulls me into his lap, nuzzling my ear with his nose. "That tickles, and your parents are right there."

"They've done this many times," he says and winks at me. "Are you having fun?"

"Absolutely. It's the perfect day to be on the lake."

"Do you want to go for a run on the tube after lunch?"

"No, thanks." I wrinkle my nose, feeling the anxiety rush up inside of me, but I act calm and collected in front of his family and my friends. "I don't think I want to get my hair wet."

"Seriously?"

"Seriously."

He frowns, watching me closely. "You brought a bag that has stuff in it for if you swim."

"I just decided I don't *want* to swim today."

Please drop this.

"But you can go if you want to. I'll watch," I continue.

"You're being silly. You're a great swimmer. Just last month, we went kayaking up at Bowman Lake, and she fell in," he tells the others, making us all laugh. "But she pulled herself right out. You're not afraid of the water."

Not that water.

The next thing I know, he's standing with me in his arms, walking to the edge of the boat.

"Don't."

"I'll go in with you."

Before I can react, he's jumped in with me in his arms, and I'm completely submerged in the water, kicking and swimming back to the surface. I immediately swim to the ladder and pull myself out of the water, on the verge of tears.

"There," he says, still treading water. "Now you're wet."

"Get out of the lake please," I say, my teeth chattering. Someone wraps a towel around my shoulders. I'm so scared, so *angry*, that I can't see anything other than Brad pulling himself out of the water.

"Not cool, man," Max mutters, but my eyes are pinned to Brad.

"What?" Brad asks. "I was just having fun with you."

"I told you I didn't want to swim."

He cocks his head to the side, narrows his eyes, and props his hands on his hips. He's not going to ask me questions in front of the others, which is a relief because I don't want to have to explain in front of the others that he just took ten years off my life.

I climb the ladder to the top deck, and hear the engine roar to life, the boat pointed to the dock.

Great. They probably want to dump me off, and I don't blame them. I'm such a downer! Not to mention, this is *not* the impression I wanted to give his parents.

What a mess.

"Hannah, will you please come inside with

Jenna and me?" Grace calls. "We want coffees and need to use the bathroom."

I sigh in relief, and climb down the ladder, not looking at Brad, and follow the girls into the house. When they head to the kitchen, I find the closest bathroom, close the door, and let myself have a meltdown.

Oh my God. I could have died. Not because of the swimming thing, but what if the electricity thing had happened again? And what if it happened when Brad was in the water and it killed *him* and I had to watch him die?

I can't do this. I can't do the relationship thing because he's going to die eventually, whether that's today or thirty years from now, and I just don't think I'm relationship material.

At all.

I'm trying to calm myself down, but now the thought of losing Brad is stuck in my head, and my heart is beating so fast I'm pretty sure I'm having a heart attack.

I take a deep breath and stare at myself in the mirror. I look ridiculous with wet red hair, pale skin, scared eyes.

Why am I always so fucking scared?

There's a knock at the door.

"Han, let me in."

I close my eyes and pray for strength. Of course Brad would follow me.

I swallow, ignore my pounding heart, and wrap myself in strength I *don't* have before opening the door and looking up at him.

"Hi. Sorry, I'm coming."

I try to brush past him, but he grips my shoulders and gently pushes me back into the bathroom, shuts the door, and cages me in against the vanity, making me look him in the eyes.

"Talk to me."

"About what?"

"You're pissing me off, Hannah."

"Yeah, well, that seems to be going around today. I need to get back to the girls."

"Fuck that, you're going to tell me what in the hell happened on that boat."

"Well, I was thrown in the water against my will and my hair got wet. No means no, Brad. I figured the chief of police would understand that."

His eyes narrow, and look a little hurt, and that just makes me feel guilty.

He didn't deserve that, and I can't look him in the eyes anymore.

"Bullshit," he says at last and tips my chin up. "This isn't about your hair. You're lying to me, and you know how I feel about that."

"Well, that's the only answer you're going to get."

I push out of his arms and march for the door,

but when I turn the knob, I pause, lowering my head in shame.

This isn't who we are.

"I'm scared," I whisper, then latch the door again and turn to face him. "I was so scared."

"Of what?"

"Of the water."

"You can swim."

"*You're not listening to me.*"

"I'm sorry." He looks genuinely baffled, which I understand. I'm baffled by me all the time. "Tell me. Make me hear you."

"I don't give a shit about my hair. And of course I can swim. It's not that I'm afraid of water, I'm afraid of *this* water. *This* lake."

I step to him, needing him to understand.

"I've been terrified all day. Actually, I've been afraid since Grace mentioned that we'd be on the boat today. All I can think about is, someone is going to dive in and get electrocuted."

"Oh, sweetheart."

"I know you said that it's okay, and I believe you. I know that you would *never* put anyone at risk, but I'm afraid of it anyway."

"Why didn't you just say something?"

"Because it's ridiculous." I feel a tear fall on my cheek, and I'm just mortified. "And I'm meeting your parents for the first time, and I want them to like me. I don't want to feel different. I know that I'm safe with you, always, but I can't get it out of my head. I do *not* want to be in that water. On the water? Fine, I can do that, but not in it. And it scared the shit out of me when you were in it because if something were to happen to you—"

"Shh," he says and pulls me against him hard, holding me so tight I don't know when I end and he begins. "Stop thinking that way. I'm not going anywhere, sweetheart. I'm right here. And if you don't want to go into the water for *any* reason, you don't have to. I'm sorry I didn't listen."

"It's not your fault. I shouldn't have said that."

"No, you're right. No means no. I don't think you're different or weird. You feel the way you feel, and that's okay."

His hand is circling firmly over my back, soothing me, and it's the best feeling in the world. I'm calmer now; the giant butterflies in my stomach are gone.

And I was in the water and survived.

"Do you want to go home?" he asks.

"Do you want me to go home?"

"Hell, no. We have prime seats for fireworks." He smiles and brushes his thumb over the apple of my cheek. "I want you to stay with us, and I want to enjoy the rest of the day with you."

"I want that too. Grace said something about iced coffees."

He chuckles and kisses my forehead, then my nose and finally my lips.

"You can have whatever you want as long as you stay."

CHAPTER TEN

Hannah

"**Y**OU CHEATED!" JENNA YELLS below us. I'm sitting on the upper deck of Grace's house, my second iced coffee sitting at my elbow, and Brad and I are listening to the others battling it out over ping pong below us.

"I had no idea that people put ping-pong tables outside," I say and laugh when Max swears ripely.

"Did you see that patio? It's huge." Brad slips his hand over mine and gives it a squeeze. "Do you feel better?"

"I do," I reply truthfully and lean in to kiss his arm. "Thanks."

"Brad!" Jacob yells up. "You need to come down here and try to beat Grace. She's beat everyone else."

"I'm fine up here," Brad calls down, but I shake my head.

"You should go play. I'm seriously great. I'm enjoying the view and my coffee."

"You're sure?"

"Completely sure."

He kisses me quickly and then hurries down to play.

"Okay, Grace, it's on," I hear him say and I smile at the sound of his voice.

I *do* feel much better. Talking to Brad helped. I should have just told him how I felt this morning, and the whole embarrassing episode never would have happened. I live too much in my own head. I overthink and it gets me in trouble.

I need to trust. To loosen up. To go with the flow.

I smirk because going with the flow is probably not something I'll ever do. But I am learning to trust.

I check my phone to make sure I haven't missed any calls from the hospital just before Mary joins me on the deck.

"Do you mind if I sit with you for a while?" she asks. I gesture to the seat that Brad just vacated and offer her a smile.

"I'd love it if you joined me."

"It's sure a beautiful day today," she says and takes a deep breath, watching the boats zip around the lake. "And this is a wonderful view."

"It sure is," I reply. "Are you from here?"

"Born and raised," she says with a nod. "I remember some Fourth of Julys that had snow."

"No way."

"A flake or two, yes. Nothing that stuck, of course. Plenty of rainy days. You just never know what you'll get around here. Where are you from, Hannah?"

"Kansas," I reply and frown. "It's very different from here."

"Yes, it is. I have a friend from Kansas. How long have you been in Cunningham Falls?"

"Just about five years." I point out a bald eagle that's swooped over the lake, looking for his dinner. "A friend of mine took a position here a few years before that, and I'd been to visit. I never considered practicing in a small town until the position came open here and Drake called me about it. And then it seemed like the best idea I'd ever heard."

"This town gets under your skin," Mary agrees. "Of course, there are pros and cons to living in a small town."

"Of course, but the pros far exceed the cons."

"I'm glad you think so," she says with a warm smile. After a quiet moment she says, "I like the way Brad looks when you're around."

"How does he look?"

"Happy. Content." She blinks rapidly, as if keeping tears at bay. "I don't know that I've ever seen him look at anyone the way he looks at you."

And, cue the butterflies again, but in a great way this time. Every woman wants to hear that the man they're in love with looks at her in a special way.

"Of course," she continues, "being married to a cop isn't easy. And being married to the chief of police is as challenging as they come."

"Oh geez," I say and laugh her off easily. "We aren't anywhere near marriage."

"Still, you're with him, and I can tell you from experience that it's a job all in itself. His hours are erratic. He sees horrible things. Some he'll tell you about, and others it's best for both of you if he doesn't. He will be tired and moody, and there will be times when it feels like he's more married to the job than he is to you.

"I know, you're not married, but I see the way you look at each other, and I know love when I see it. You haven't said it yet, have you?"

I shake my head no and she keeps talking.

"That's okay. It's good to take it easy and let your relationship progress naturally. But you need to know going into it that you're not just in a relationship with a man. He's an important man, and in this town in particular, they will feel like they own him. You'll share him.

"The statistics for marriages lasting for cops aren't good."

"Mary, I mean no disrespect, but I'm going to interrupt you for a moment." I hold my hand up and when she stops, I shake my head. "I know who he is. And I would like to add that as a doctor, my schedule is just as erratic. I see horrible things. And my patients do believe they own me, and that

I should be at their beck and call. I get it. I like to think that I get it as much as anyone who isn't a cop can."

"You're right," she says, watching me carefully. "You would, wouldn't you? You know, my Bruce's daddy was also an officer here in Cunningham Falls, and his mom tried to warn me about these things right before we got married. I didn't listen to her. I was so in love with that man I couldn't see straight."

"And it seems to have worked out well for you," I point out.

"Forty years of marriage," she says with a nod. "Forty years, and only the past three of them have been somewhat normal. But I wouldn't have traded it. What he did was important. He kept people safe, and he saved lives. I'm so proud of him. When Brad told us that he'd applied for the chief position when Bruce announced his retirement, I tried to talk him out of it. I knew that if he wanted a family it would take a toll. But he's so much like his father." She shrugs as if to say, *what are you going to do?* "He's doing a good job, and we are so proud of him."

"I am, too."

Her head whips around to stare at me for a moment and then she smiles. "I think you mean that."

"Of course I do. He's an amazing man. I'm damn proud of him, and I'm enjoying spending time with him very much. I don't know what the future holds for us, but I'm going to continue to enjoy him, for as long as I can. No relationship is easy, and we both chose professions that are harder than most, but I also think that means that we're dedicated. I don't see why that wouldn't also include being dedicated to each other."

"I like you, Hannah." Mary is smiling now, almost smugly.

"Really? Because it sounds like you're trying to warn me away from your son."

"Not at all. I just wanted to see what you're made of. I think you can stick up for yourself just fine. Not just to me, but more importantly, to the townspeople. You'll need that backbone where they're concerned."

"They don't scare me," I reply honestly.

"Good."

"Don't scare her off already," Brad says as he joins us. "I defeated Grace, but it wasn't pretty."

"He did not," Grace yells up to us, making us all laugh.

"When are the fireworks?" I ask, looking at the time. "It doesn't get dark here until after ten."

"They wait until then," Brad says. "I have to have my radio on, just in case. I have sheriff deputies helping my guys tonight, but if anything major happens, they might need to reach me."

"I get it," I reply. "What do we do in the mean time?"

"Eat," Jacob says from the doorway. "I've just had more food brought in."

"I'm going to gain twenty pounds today." I laugh and jump up from my chair. "But I'm not complaining. Also, I think I'll go down and kick some ass at the ping pong."

"You think you can beat me?" Brad asks with a sexy brow cocked.

"Hell, yes, I can beat you. And Grace, too."

"Let's do it," Brad says and rubs his hands together. I follow him down to the patio below where everyone else is hanging out, eating fresh Mexican food from a local restaurant.

"How did you have this delivered on a holiday?" I ask Jacob, immediately reaching for a plate.

"I own the restaurant, darling," he replies smugly and steals a chip off of his wife's plate.

"That'll do it." I load my plate with tacos and chips, gratefully accept a Mexican Coke from Max, and take a seat next to Jenna. "This smells *so good.*"

"Sm gmmf," Jenna says with her mouth full, making me grin.

The food isn't just *good*, it's to die for, and I eat more than my share. When I can't shove another bite into my mouth, I stand, stretch my arms over my head, then saunter over to the ping-pong table and pick up a paddle.

"Let's do this, Hull."

He's sitting on the couch, watching me with hot green eyes. The kind of hot that tells me he wants to bend me over this table and do things to me that are definitely *not* appropriate for mixed company.

I toss him a sassy grin. "Well? Are you coming?"

"I'm coming," he says, his lips twitching with humor. "I just worry about this."

"Why?"

"I don't want to embarrass you in front of our friends."

"Aww, aren't you sweet?" I stick my lower lip out in a pout, bat my eyelashes. "So chivalrous."

"Just looking out for you, sweetheart."

"Thanks, but I've got this."

I serve the ball perfectly, and he volleys it back, but he's no match for my backhand, and he misses my next shot. He whips those hot green eyes up to mine and looks genuinely surprised.

"You're good."

"I know."

I serve again, and before long I win, not even giving him a chance to score on me.

"Who's next?"

"Me!" Grace jumps up, stretches her arms across her body, and takes the paddle from Brad, who is scratching his head and watching me like he doesn't know me at all.

Which only makes me laugh.

"How did you get so good at this?" Grace asks

as she serves the ball and I volley it back to her. We volley back and forth more than a dozen times before she gets the point.

Grace is *good* at this.

"College," I reply. "I didn't play beer pong, I played ping pong."

After a ferocious match, I win by just two points.

"You are a worthy opponent," Grace says, bowing before me.

"As are you," I reply, bowing in return, and then we dissolve in a fit of giggles, hugging each other. "How did *you* get so good?"

"I practice a lot. I may be clumsy, but this seems to be one of the things I'm good at."

"I'll play with you anytime." I give her a high five and then head straight for the food again. "Ping pong makes me hungry."

"I have dessert coming down soon," Grace says as I take a bite of a chip. "Cheesecake."

"Good lord," Jenna moans, covering her belly. "Give me thirty minutes to get this food baby to settle."

"Same," Max says. "And then bring it on."

The rest of the evening is full of laughter, ping pong, and food. Stolen kisses. Conversation.

I notice both of Brad's parents watching us closely, but kindly, throughout the hours that follow. It's a relief to know that his mother likes me.

I mean, we're grown adults, but having their approval means a lot.

Suddenly, just before ten, Brad's radio goes off.

"They're going to start the light show," Brad says.

"Let's go up to the deck," Grace says with excitement. We follow her up and all lean against the railing.

Brad walks up behind me and wraps his arms around me, caging me against the railing. Just as the first fireworks burst into the sky, he lays his lips against my ear.

"Thank you," he murmurs as the others ooh and aah over the lights in the sky.

"For what?"

"This. All of this."

He kisses my cheek, and then we're silent, watching the sky light up, surrounded by those closest to us.

It's been the best day that I've had in a *very* long time.

Maybe ever.

"The boss man wants a word," my nurse, Melissa, says. She's poked her head around the doorjamb of my office. We had a long one today, and it's only late morning.

"You look tired."

"I am," she says with a shrug. "I hate it when the fourth falls on a week day."

"I know." I smile, feeling the effects from being up late last night myself. "Thankfully our patient load is light today."

She nods and offers me a grin. "You have a patient in room four, and then you're done until after lunch."

"Cool." I grab my stethoscope and my computer. "I'll go talk to Jim and then see my patient. This shouldn't take long."

She nods and I walk to Jim's office. He calls me inside.

"Hi there," I say and sit in the chair in front of his desk.

"Good morning," he replies with a kind smile. Jim has been an OB/GYN in Cunningham Falls for forty years. He's no longer delivering babies, but he's still the head doctor in this practice, and I respect him immensely. I've learned so much from him since I came on. "Hannah, we need to talk."

"Okay."

"I've decided that it's time for you to stop taking call 24/7."

I sit quietly, blinking at him, sure I've heard him wrong.

"Did you hear me?"

"I don't think so."

He repeats himself, and I frown. "I don't understand. Have I done something wrong?"

"Not yet," he says and takes his glasses off, rubbing his eyes. "But you work too much, Hannah. There will be no more taking call on your nights off."

"My patients hire *me* to be there when their babies are born, Jim. It's important to them that I follow through with their care from beginning to end."

"I get it," he says, raising his hands in surrender. "I know what you're saying. But Hannah, we have five perfectly capable doctors in this clinic who can all deliver babies. It's too much for you to work twenty-four, sometimes forty-eight hours in a row, and then show up here to take appointments as well. You'll burn yourself out before you're forty, and I won't allow that."

"I didn't realize that being dedicated to my job was punishable," I reply, feeling my whole body tighten defensively.

"I'm not punishing you, Hannah." He sighs and watches me for a moment. "You're a wonderful doctor, and having you on staff has only strengthened this clinic. I value your education and your knowledge. But you put in too many hours. One day, it won't be *safe*. You'll miss a step out of pure exhaustion, and I have to think about the welfare of you and our patients. I'm not telling you that you can't work. I'm telling you that you can't work on your days off."

"Which is kind of the same thing," I reply. "I

love this job. This is who I am."

"No. This is what you do." He smiles kindly and leans back in his chair. "In fact, I've been looking back over your schedule, and it's come to my attention that you haven't taken vacation time in two years."

"I was going to last summer, but Dr. Preston had her car accident and I had to fill in for her."

"I remember." He nods. "And it was appreciated. I want you to make up for it this year."

"Okay."

"Today."

"Excuse me?"

"Beginning today, I want you to take that week's vacation, paid. In addition to the other vacation time you have coming this year."

I frown. "Jim, I have two patients ready to have babies in the next few weeks."

"And if they go into labor, there are doctors here to do that, Hannah."

"So, I have to take a week off of work."

He laughs. "No, you *get* to take a week. Starting now."

"I have a patient in a room."

"Already been taken care of," he says. "We help each other around here. We're cool like that."

"I'm sorry, are you sure I haven't done something wrong?"

"No." He shakes his head and holds my gaze with wise grey eyes. "You're an excellent doctor, and I want you to be here for many years. The rest of your career, if I can manage it. And to do that, I need to protect you from burning yourself out."

"What am I supposed to do with all of this time?" I ask.

"That's up to you," he says and laughs when I just stare at him, dumbfounded. "Hannah, this is a good thing. You'll have more time to live your life."

"Huh." I narrow my eyes on him. "If you're really trying to squeeze me out of here, I'll put up a fight."

"I hope so. Now, you don't have to go home, but you can't stay here. Not until next Wednesday."

"But it's Tuesday."

"Exactly. You'll be off from this Tuesday until next Wednesday. A whole week."

"I guess I could hike," I reply, thinking out loud.

"Yes, that sounds great. Take a trip. Go hike. Go camping. Hell, go to Europe, I don't care. Just don't come here."

"You're going to miss me," I promise him, and he rolls his eyes.

"It's a week, Hannah."

Might as well be a month.

CHAPTER ELEVEN

Hannah

I'M SORRY TO BUG you at work," Abby says on the phone twenty minutes later just as I walk in my house, "but I have a question."

"I'm not at work."

"What? Why?"

"What's your question?"

"Right." She clears her throat. "I have an extra pair of concert tickets to see Maroon5 next month, and I'm wondering if you'd like to go?"

"Is this really a question? Of course I want to go."

"Cool. Now, why are you not at work?"

I sigh and pull a bottle of water out of the fridge. "Because I was sent home." I sit and tell her everything that Jim just said. "I mean, what am I supposed to do for a whole week?"

"Are you kidding me?"

I frown at the phone. "No, I'm not kidding. A whole week? What the hell?"

"Hannah, you're supposed to *relax*. Have fun. I've wanted you to do this for *years*. I can hear how tired you always are. I think it's awesome that Jim wants you to have a normal life."

"I'm a doctor," I remind her. "We don't have normal lives."

"Well, now you can."

"It's a lot of time to fill. I don't know what to do."

"I can think of a dozen things. Go to the movies, a short road trip, get a massage. Get your nails done. Schedule happy hours with your friends. But first, I think you should go buy lunch for that sexy police chief of yours and take it to him. That would be fun."

"That's not a bad idea." I turn the idea over in my head, and feel a grin spread over my face. "I'm actually kind of hungry."

"See? You'll find things to do. If you can't think of anything, text me and I'll help."

"Okay." I laugh, and grab my handbag. "Thanks for inviting me to the concert. Send me the details."

"Will do. Now, go feed your cop, and then maybe have sexy time in his office."

She hangs up, and I'm suddenly excited to be off of work for the day. I swing into *Little Deli* and chat with Mrs. Blakely while I wait for our sandwiches to be made, and then drive over to the station.

As I'm walking inside, a moment of doubt creeps in. I didn't call ahead. What if he's not available? Or not here at all.

I should have called.

But when I walk inside, I see Brad standing by his assistant, giving her a folder, and he glances up, smiling when he sees me.

"Hey," he says as I approach.

"Hi. I brought lunch."

"Really? I'm starving. No calls, please."

He shows me into his office, closes the door behind us, and pulls me in for a long, hot kiss. The kind of kiss that makes me forget about everything else.

The kind of kiss that makes a girl's panties wet.

"What was that for?" I whisper when he pulls away.

"Lunch." He winks, then takes the bag from my hands and leads me to a sitting area in the corner of his office. There's a loveseat, a chair, and a coffee table. "I thought you worked today."

"I thought so too."

For the second time in less than an hour, I relay the conversation with Jim and then bite into my turkey on rye, moody all over again.

"I think it's fantastic."

"Everyone thinks it's fantastic except me. I don't need a week off."

"Maybe it'll feel good," he suggests and pulls the tomatoes off of his sandwich. *No tomatoes.* This whole learning someone else thing is way more complex than I ever imagined.

"I just don't know what I'm supposed to do with so much down time," I reply and then shrug. "I guess I can repaint my bathroom or something."

"You'll fill the time," he says with more confidence than I feel. "And you can spend this evening with me."

"I can't." I shrug when his eyes whip up to mine. "It's grand opening night at the new dress shop downtown, and we're making a girls'night out of it."

"Grace and Jenna?" he asks.

"Yep, and I'm actually excited for it. We don't do it often."

"Cool," he says and keeps eating his sandwich. When he's finished, I straddle his lap and kiss him hard, wrapping my arms around his neck. His big hands slide over my sides and to my ass. "I'm not fucking you twenty feet from my guys," he says, breathing hard.

"I just want to cuddle," I reply. "Get your head out of the gutter."

"Sweetheart, you've pressed that sweet pussy of yours against my cock. My head is squarely planted in the gutter until you move. Not that I want you to do that."

"I just wanted to feel you," I say and hug him

close. "And to thank you for being so laid back. So calm. So *steady*."

"That's sexy." I can hear the smile in his voice.

"Actually, it is sexy." I pull back to look in his eyes. "You always keep it together, and you don't get angry over silly things like girls' night out."

"I would be an asshole if I did that."

"I've known some assholes," I reply. "And I'm just glad that you're *not*. So thank you."

"You're welcome."

"Also, I'd like to come to your house later after time with the girls, if you don't mind."

"I don't mind," he replies and pulls me down for a long, sweet kiss. His lips are soft, but they know exactly what they're doing as they take command of mine in a lazy, sexy dance. "In fact, I'd very much enjoy your company tonight."

"It's settled then." I grin and climb off of him, then gaze around his office, looking for something specific.

"What are you looking for?"

"Handcuffs."

I glance down at him, catching the raised eyebrow.

"I think you should bring some of those home with you."

"Do you?"

"Oh yeah. That would be fun."

A smile spreads over his sexy lips, and I can't help but lean in to kiss him again, enjoying the smell of him, and the way his face feels in my hands.

But if I keep this up, we really will fuck twenty feet away from his guys.

So I back away and gather the mess from lunch, toss it away, and retrieve my handbag. "I'll see you later, then. I guess I'll go clean my closet."

"See? You're already getting projects done."

"I'd rather be delivering babies."

I shrug and wave, then leave his office. Maybe he's right. Maybe it'll be a good week. It sure was nice to be able to bring Brad lunch in the middle of the day.

And I have girls' night out tonight, without being on call, so that's a bonus. I can relax and enjoy without worrying about being called in for a delivery or an emergency.

I don't remember the last time that happened.

And, just for shits and giggles, I'm going to take Abby's advice and schedule a massage for this week.

Maybe everyone's right. Maybe this week won't be so boring after all.

"This place is *so* great," Jenna says shortly after we walk into *Dress It Up*, the new clothing boutique owned by her friend, Willa. Jenna is perfectly dressed today in a short sun dress with a fun hat and strappy heeled sandals. She looks like she walked out of a freaking magazine.

"She has beautiful things," I agree and smile when a beautiful, tall brunette comes walking toward us. She pulls Jenna in for a big hug.

"I'm so happy you're here," Willa says. "I was afraid no one would come."

"Why? This is the *best*," Grace says, also hugging Willa. "And this is our friend, Hannah Malone, who is also the best."

"I've heard your name around town," Willa says, shaking my hand. "It's nice to finally meet you."

"You as well," I reply. "Your shop is lovely."

And I'm not just being polite. The place is *magical.* She's gone with a grey, white, black, and pink theme. The floors are reclaimed barn wood. Chandeliers dripping with crystal hang above us. It's the epitome of fancy, stylish, and just flat out *pretty.*

"Thanks," she says with a smile and glances around. "It's been one big project, but I'm happy with it. I have clothing lines from New York and London, as well as some smaller labels that I love. And let's not forget the shoes."

"No, let's not," Jenna says with a laugh. "Shoes are my love language."

"Do you have flats for those of us who might kill ourselves otherwise?" Grace asks hopefully.

"Of course," Willa replies. "There's something in this store for everyone. There's wine floating around, along with some light appetizers. Help yourselves, and have fun. That's the most important thing. And let me know if you have any questions." Willa waves at another group of women who just walked in. "Excuse me, ladies."

"She's nice," I say as I watch her walk away. "Why did Max dump her?"

"Because he's stupid," Jenna says, handing me a can of Coke. But I surprise her by shaking my head and reaching for the wine. "You never drink."

"I do tonight. I'm not on call, so guess what? I can." I take a sip and enjoy not feeling guilty about having fun. "Let's browse, ladies."

"Let's spend some money," Grace corrects me, and we begin to wander through the shop, enjoying the beautiful things Willa has for sale.

"I love living in a small town, but it's so hard to shop," I say and pull a summer dress off the rack. "It's nice to have a trendy place in town."

"You're *so* right," Jenna replies and points to the garment in my hand. "That dress is a must buy."

I nod and drape it over my arm.

Over the next hour, we drink more glasses of wine, and make piles of clothes that we're going to buy.

It's fucking amazing, and so damn fun.

"This bikini is *everything*," Jenna says, showing me a turquoise two-piece.

"It will look amazing with your hair," I agree, then show her a T-shirt that says *Coffee Before Talkie*. "I need this."

"Oh yes, that's completely you," Jenna replies with a laugh. "And look at this one!"

I Don't Trip, I Do Random Gravity Checks.

"That's Grace," I say, adding it to my pile. She has to have it.

"She needs this one too," Jenna says, showing me a T-shirt that says *Rocking The Spoiled Wife Life*.

"Yes, perfect."

"Hannah," Grace says loudly, rushing from across the store, holding something in her hand. "You have to smell this."

But before I can, Grace trips on her feet, falling right into me, and knocking her head against my cheek, making me see stars. On my way down, she grabs my arm, trying to keep me up, but we both end up on the floor, a tangle of arms and legs, and glitter falling from the air.

"Oh shit," she says, snorting. "I hope I didn't ruin any clothes."

"You just ruined me," I reply. We're both giggling like crazy.

"Did I hurt your face?"

"I don't think so." I touch around my eye with my fingertips. It's a little sore, but not bad. "Are you hurt?"

"Nah." She shakes her head, and glitter falls out of her hair. "That was a bath bomb, by the way."

"It exploded."

We look at each other and dissolve into giggles again.

"Willa's going to be *pissed*," Grace says.

"No, I'm not," Willa says from behind us. "Just don't touch anything else with all of that glitter all over you."

We look at each other and laugh some more. We laugh so hard that I can't catch my breath. My sides ache, I can barely breathe, but I can't stop laughing.

We look ridiculous.

Finally, once we've all paid for our things, and left *Dress It Up*, we stand on the sidewalk, wiping the tears from under our eyes.

"That wine was *strong*," I say, once I catch my breath.

"And you never drink, so your tolerance is low," Jenna replies. "You probably shouldn't drive."

I stare at her for a moment, and realize there are two of her.

"No, definitely no driving for me. I'll walk."

"It's raining," Grace says. I glance around and then rush out from under the awning, letting the rain fall on me.

"Oh, it's nice."

"She's so drunk," Jenna says to Grace, making me laugh.

"I'm not *that* drunk."

Okay. I am.

"We can take you home."

"I'm not going home." I shake my head and turn a circle in the rain, but then I'm dizzy so I stop and just let the water fall on me.

"Where are you going?"

"To Brad's." I smile at Jenna. "I know you don't want to hear this, but I'm going to have some seriously hot sex with him tonight."

"Good for you," Jenna says and then wrinkles her nose. "Ew."

"Nope, it's not *ew*. It's *wow*. It's *holy shit, I didn't even know my pussy did that*."

"Holy shit, she's funny drunk," Grace says, laughing. "Come on, drunk girl. We'll drive you to Brad's."

"Actually, I really do want to walk," I reply. "Don't look at me like that. I'll be fine. I'm really not that drunk, and it's not cold."

"I don't know," Jenna says. "Brad would kill me if he knew I let you walk to his place when you're like this."

"I won't let him kill you. I swear." I hug them both, then wave as I begin my walk to Brad's house. It's only about a mile from downtown. I can certainly walk a mile.

But when I get about halfway there, the sun decides to go down. So now I'm walking in the rain *and* the dark.

But I don't care.

I love it here. I love my friends, and I love my boyfriend.

And I love the rain.

The rain that is currently falling even harder. So hard that it's difficult to see in front of me, so I duck under the branches of a big maple tree and wait for a few minutes, hoping it'll die down a bit.

It doesn't rain a whole lot in the summer in Montana, so when it does, it's warm and fast. This will pass.

"Are you okay out there?" Someone yells out from their house.

"I'm fine, just waiting for a break in the rain," I call out in return. This must be a good answer because they don't say anything more.

Finally, the rain calms to a heavy sprinkle, so I set out to Brad's house again. Rather than just dusk, it's pitch dark when I make it to his house. The front windows are lit from inside, with the shades pulled. His porch light is on.

I wander up the sidewalk, climb the two steps to his porch, and then sit in his porch chair, breathing deeply.

I'm almost sober now, but I want to be all the way sober when he opens the door. I don't need to make an ass out of myself in front of him.

No way.

After three deep breaths, I stand and knock on his door, excited to see him. I'm not prepared to see the expression of horror on his face when he swings the door open.

CHAPTER TWELVE

Brad

I'M PATHETIC.

I've spent all evening doing my best to stay busy, waiting for Hannah to ring the doorbell, trying to keep my mind off of her and on other things. I paid bills, I finished hanging some cabinets in my garage, and I gave Sadie a bath.

Much to her dismay.

I've had music playing through the house as I putter around, pretending that I'm not thinking about Hannah and her beautiful blue eyes. Her perfect skin. The way she laughs when we're being silly, or the way she moans when I'm making her crazy.

But as soon as I'm distracted by something, my mind wanders back to her, and I can't help but wonder what she's doing and why in the hell she's not here yet.

Just as I finish folding a load of laundry, there's a knock on the front door. I grin and hurry over, swing it open, and standing before me is Hannah.

Soaking wet.

Covered in glitter.

A black eye.

Anger, swift and hot, surges through me, but before I can ask who the hell did this to her, she smiles brightly and says, "Oh my God, I had *so much fun.*"

She walks past me into the living room, drops her shopping bags and purse on my couch, and greets an excited Sadie, giving the dog pets and kisses, transferring the glitter to the clean animal.

"Hannah."

"Yeah?" She swings around to look at me. "Oh, sorry. I should have done this first."

She launches herself in my arms and kisses me soundly, twisting her fingers in the hair at the back of my neck.

"You smell good," she murmurs.

"You… *don't.*" I laugh and set her down. "Have you been drinking?"

"Oh yeah," she replies with a snort. "I didn't have to work, so I had some wine."

"And you drove here?"

She immediately scowls. "Hell no, I don't have my car. I walked here. I'm not my father."

"Oh, I'm sorry. Of course." I'm completely thrown. This is so unlike Hannah, I'm not sure how to react. But she looks happy, so there's that. "Who the fuck had their hands on you?"

"Huh?"

"The black eye."

She frowns and feels her face, and then laughs again. "Oh, that was Grace. She likes it rough." She snorts again, dissolving in laughter. "It doesn't hurt."

"I can't believe Jenna let you walk here," I mutter, but Hannah shakes her head.

"I insisted. It felt good." She shivers. "But now I'm getting cold."

"You need a hot shower." I take her hand and lead her into my bathroom. I turn on the water to heat up, then turn to her and have the pleasure of stripping her bare. "You even have glitter in your navel."

"Now I don't have to have it pierced."

She's grinning from ear to ear. "I'm glad you had fun, sweetheart."

"I had more than fun." She grips onto my shoulders to steady herself as I pull her wet panties down her legs. "I had a blast. We shopped a ton, and I met some new people. How is it that I've lived here for five years, and there are still so many people I don't know?"

I guide her into the shower and shut the glass door, still listening to her talk.

"I should know more people," she continues.

"But I work too much. It feels good to finally feel like I'm part of this community."

"You *are* a part of the community."

"You're sweet." She clears the fog from the glass and smiles out at me. "Brad?"

"Yes, Hannah."

"Can you please come in here and help me wash this glitter off?" She bats her eyelashes, making me grin. "Pretty please?"

I'll never say no to getting naked with her. Ever.

"If I come in there, it may not stop at washing glitter."

"Oh good."

I hurry out of my clothes and join her. "What do you need?"

"Besides you?"

"Yes." She passes me the washcloth that she's soaped up.

"I think my back is dirty." She spins around, and she's right. There's glitter everywhere, so I get to work, washing it off, then rinsing the cloth, over and over again until it's gone. She turns around and points to her breasts, not saying a word. I lather fresh soap on the cloth and wash her chest, her belly and sides, and then she bites her lip and points to her neck.

"I don't see any glitter there."

"It's there," she replies. Her breathing is faster

as I drag the wet cloth over her neck. I push her out of the water and against the wall, and she surprises me by resting her foot up on the bench and points to her inner thigh. "Right there."

Wordlessly, I wash her inner thighs, up to the crease of her legs, not touching her pussy.

"Brad," she says.

"Mm hm."

"Right here." She points to her center, and I immediately lower to my knees, staring in awe at the beauty of her. Her clit is swollen with desire, as are her lips, and I've never wanted someone so bad in my damn life.

Rather than use the washcloth, I lean in and lick her, from pussy to clit and back again, before pulling her lips into my mouth and sucking.

"Harder," she says, panting. I comply, using my teeth a bit as well, and she's writhing against the wall as she grabs my hair in a death grip. I push her leg up higher, sure to keep her balanced with my other hand and go to town on her, licking and sucking, biting and nibbling until she cries out in absolute pleasure.

I stand and boost her up against the wall, then push inside her. "You're so fucking wet."

"Turned on," she mutters and squeezes herself around me. "You turn me the hell on, Brad Hull."

I grin against her neck and pound her against the wall, unable to go slow or soft. Slow or soft doesn't fit our mood tonight. We're ravenous, and

I'm going to take and take until neither of us can stand it anymore.

"Can't get enough of you."

"Good."

She bites my shoulder, and that's it. I can't do this against the wall anymore, so I flip off the water, and carry her, dripping wet, to my guest room, lay her down and continue to feast on her. Her tits, her pussy, every bit of her.

And she's giving it back just as fiercely. Her hips buck, her hands grab, and she's kissing and biting every piece of flesh she can find.

It's like we're crazy animals, unable to stop consuming each other.

I pull out and flip her over, slap her ass, and plunge inside again, fucking her until we're both crying out, coming hard.

And when we're done, I carry her back to my bed, tuck us both in and begin again, unable to keep my hands off of her.

"I'm sober now," she says with a lazy smile and opens up for me beautifully. "And thank goodness. I definitely want to remember this tomorrow."

"We should sleep at some point tonight," Hannah says a few hours later. We're in the kitchen, making pancakes.

"You said you're hungry."

"I am." She grins and passes me the eggs. She's sitting on the counter, wearing one of my CFPD T-shirts, her hair a riot of red. She's adorable. "But you have to work in the morning."

"I've survived on little sleep before."

Once the batter is mixed, I set to work pouring it on my skillet. While I wait for it to be ready to flip, I settle between her thighs at the counter and kiss her soundly. "You're damn gorgeous, Hannah."

"I must be a mess," she says, wrinkling her nose. "I don't think we got all the glitter off."

"I'll be cleaning glitter out of my house for weeks."

"I'm sorry."

"It's okay. It'll bring back happy memories every time."

She drags her fingertips down my face and her expression is suddenly serious.

"What is it?"

She shakes her head and breaks eye contact, looking at my hair as she runs her fingers through it.

I take her hand in mine and kiss her palm, then lay it against my cheek.

"Talk to me, Han."

It's quiet in the house. Dark, aside from the lights under the cabinets, setting the room in a low glow.

"You need to flip the pancakes," she says and kisses my forehead before I move to the skillet and give them a flip. But before I can return to her, she jumps off the counter and retrieves two plates, the butter, and syrup, and the moment from a few moments ago is lost.

"I can't believe how hungry I am," she says.

"These three are ready."

"Gimme."

I put the pancakes on her plate and then pour two more for me, and turn to watch her slather butter and syrup all over her middle of the night snack.

"These are so good," she says after taking a big bite. "Who knew sex could make a girl so hungry?"

"I'd better stock up on pancake mix."

She winks at me, her mouth full.

"I plan to keep you *starving*."

"Right on."

When mine are finished, I turn off the skillet and join her at the table to eat with her. It's a simple thing, having an after sex snack with her, but it's intimate. It makes me feel closer to her.

I glance up in time to see her eyes are heavy.

"I think we've finally worn you out."

She smiles softly. "Yeah. I'm tired."

"What's wrong?" I ask when she frowns.

"I have a bit of a headache. I hope I'm not developing migraines."

I just shake my head and take my last bite. "You drank too much, that's all."

"Hmm."

We put our dishes in the sink and I lead her to my bed, anxious to feel her skin on skin again.

"Why do you always think that something's wrong?" I ask softly.

She thinks about it for a moment, her eyes closed.

"Because I know too much. About medicine. That's what Drake says, anyway."

"What do *you* think?"

"I think that it's part of the anxiety. I worry." She yawns. "I don't think I've ever talked about this with anyone except Drake, and even he only knows a little of it."

"I want to know everything about you," I reply honestly. "Not to judge you, but to learn you."

"I know. I feel the same." She turns on her side and looks up at me. "Why does it always feel safer to talk about things in the dark?"

"Because we feel hidden here. Safe."

"I guess so." She scoots closer to me and threads her leg through mine. "I've always been a worrier. I don't remember a time when I wasn't. It's probably a chemical imbalance. The anxiety, I mean. And there are meds I can take, but it's been there for so long, I'm pretty good at managing it."

"Hiding it," I correct her.

"Tomato, tomahto," she says with a smile. "Either way, I don't feel like I need medicine. But there are going to be times that I'll think I'm sick. Or that I have a disease. I'll always wonder. I've asked colleagues to do full body scans before, just to give me peace of mind, but they usually laugh me off."

"Sweetheart," I murmur and kiss her forehead. "You're a strong, healthy woman."

"I know. The rational side of me *knows* that. I have no reason to believe otherwise. It's like the bear thing, or the lake thing the other day. I *know* better, but I can't change the thoughts."

"I see."

"No, you don't. And that's okay. I'd rather you didn't understand. But I appreciate you asking and not judging."

"Can you tell me more about your parents?"

She frowns, but then shrugs. "Sure. What do you want to know?"

"You just didn't say too much, other than your father killed your mother in an accident, and you haven't seen him since."

"That's pretty much it."

"But that doesn't give me much information."

"You could run his record," she replies.

Oh, I have.

"That's not personal either," I remind her.

She sighs. "I honestly don't think of him. Ever. I know that sounds heartless, but he wasn't a great father, or even a nice person. At least, not that I remember. I remember him being drunk most of the time. He didn't work because he couldn't hold a job. Mom stressed out about money and me and everything else, and he just drank.

"I spent a lot of time with Abby and her parents, or at my friends' homes. I preferred it, actually. He never hurt me. He didn't hit me, or yell at me. He ignored me."

"Sometimes that's just as bad," I reply, wanting to wrap her in my arms and protect her.

"I agree. I didn't really consider him at all, until the accident. I didn't think of him as dangerous. He was more of a pain in the ass.

"My mom was pretty great. She was soft spoken. I have her hair and eyes, and I'm grateful for that. I don't know what it would be like to look in the mirror and see *him*."

"I'm sure she was beautiful."

"She was." She smiles sweetly. "And she made the best cookies. She was a great cook. I didn't inherit that ability."

"Too bad."

She wrinkles her nose in that adorable way she does. "Yeah, too bad. Her name was Vivienne, and she wasn't even forty when she died."

"Did she often ride with your dad after he'd been drinking?"

"Not that I know of. They didn't do much of anything together. I wasn't home that day. I decided to spend most of the winter break with Abby, and we were having a New Year's Eve party at her house with some of our friends. Mom had called earlier in the day to say hello and to check in, like she usually did. That's the last time I spoke to her. I was impatient to get off the phone so I could help decorate for the party.

"At about three in the morning, a few cops came to my aunt and uncle's house, and they sat us all down and told me that my mom was gone."

"I've had to go on too many of those calls."

She nods. "It must suck."

"It does."

"I miss her. She would have been proud of me, and she probably would have moved to Montana with me."

"And you never heard from your father after that?"

"Why would I? He never paid attention to me before, there's no reason that I would after. I didn't go to the trial. He plead no contest, so his sentence would be more lenient."

"Thank you for sharing all of this with me."

"You're welcome. And now we don't have to talk about it again."

She yawns and snuggles into me, burying her face in my neck. Before long, she's breathing with the even, steady breaths of sleep, and I'm still turning the story over in my head. I don't feel bad for her; she wouldn't want that. But I wish she'd had a better father in her life.

It's amazing to me that she's as healthy as she is, given the circumstances of her childhood.

She's strong. And brave. And she's mine.

Sadie meets me at the door at lunchtime. I walk inside and find a glassy-eyed Hannah sitting on the couch, staring at nothing in particular. She's wearing my T-shirt again, and Sadie returns to her side.

"Hi there," I say, and she looks up at me and offers me a small smile.

"Hi."

"Are you just waking up?"

"Yeah." She pets Sadie's head. "Don't judge me. I haven't had a hangover since I was twenty-one."

"You had a lot of fun last night."

"Yeah, and then I was up fucking for the rest of it." Her eyes light up when she sees the coffee in my hand. "Is that for me?"

"Of course." I pass it to her. "This is too. It's a breakfast sandwich."

"You're really good to me." She takes a sip of her coffee, closes her eyes, and smiles. "This is nice. Thank you."

"You're welcome."

"Were you on time for work this morning?"

"Of course," I say and scoop her up in my arms, then sit and settle her in my lap. "I'm never late."

"You were up all night, too." She sips her coffee and then lays her head on my shoulder. "Should I feel guilty?"

"For what?"

"For your lack of sleep."

I chuckle and kiss her head, smelling her hair. "No. It's my own fault for not being able to keep my hands off of you."

"You always say sweet things. And you do sweet things. You're just a sweet man, Brad."

"Don't let it get out. I have a reputation to protect."

"Ah yes, your badass Chief Sexypants reputation."

"Sexywhat?"

"Sexypants. It's your name when you're not around."

I stare down at her in surprise. "That's what you call me when I'm not around?"

"Only to Jenna and Grace, and not all the time." She grins and kisses my chin. "Don't be mad. It's a complimentary nickname."

"If you say so."

"I'm glad you're here. It's easier to wake up

when you're here rather than by myself."

"Well, you have me for about twenty more minutes. Then I have to go back to work."

"Already?"

"It's noon, Hannah. I can't take the rest of the day off."

"What am I going to do all afternoon?"

"Take Sadie for a walk."

She sips her coffee, giving it thought. "I do need to go get my car."

"I can drive you to your car."

"Nah. Sadie and I will walk to get it. I'll do the walk of shame." She smiles. "I've never done that before."

"I guess there's a first for everything."

She laughs and settles against me, and it feels like heaven to just hold her in my arms for a moment, enjoying the calm.

"How is work today?"

"Busy. There was a home break in last night, and a car accident this morning, with one fatality."

Her arm squeezes my shoulder. "I'm sorry."

"Me, too. So, I'll be busy this afternoon."

"What do you have planned for this evening?" she asks.

"I'm open."

"Good. I'd like to treat you to dinner."

"We've discussed this. I buy dinner."

She rolls her eyes. "Fine, I'd like to go out for dinner."

"Done."

"You're difficult."

"You just told me yesterday that I'm easy going and steady."

"Until you're difficult."

CHAPTER THIRTEEN

Hannah

I'VE CLEANED THE HOUSE. Sadie and I walked to town to get my car.

I even cooked dinner.

Brad should be home any minute, and I feel about as domestic as I ever have in my life. I'm not sure how I feel about it. I mean, I feel good about it, but it's new. Should I be wearing an apron? Should I be naked *except* for the apron?

That would make him smile.

But then dinner would go cold because I'm quite sure he'd fuck me against the kitchen counter. I'd be disappointed if he didn't.

So I'll keep my clothes on for now.

Also, why am I overthinking this? It's dinner. And by dinner, I mean chicken enchiladas that I slapped together because like I told him last night, I'm not a great cook.

It's not a big deal.

The door to the garage opens, and Brad comes

in, smiling, carrying a baby carrier.

I do a double take, and then frown.

"I knew it."

"What?" He sets the carrier on the table and begins pulling blankets off of it, unearthing an adorable, dark-haired baby girl.

"I told Grace that I was sure that you had a secret baby somewhere."

He just laughs and shakes his head as he pulls the baby into his arms and turns to face me. His eyes are soft, almost dewy, as he looks down at the little one. "She isn't mine."

"That's a relief. And she isn't *mine* because I definitely haven't had a baby. So whose is she?"

"My detective's little girl. Her name is Megan." He smiles at her and she reaches for Brad's nose.

"She's cute." I cross my arms over my chest, keeping a safe distance between me and them. "Why is she with you?"

"Her daddy wanted to take his wife out for dinner, but the babysitter cancelled, so I volunteered to take her."

"It's like I don't even know you," I reply and laugh. "This might be the very last thing I would expect."

"She loves me," he says in defense. "Look."

At that moment, Megan stretches her arms out to me, whimpering.

"Or, she's trying to escape."

"You can take her," he suggests, and I freeze.

"That's okay."

"She's asking for you."

I walk to the oven and open it, retrieving the enchiladas. "I'm finishing dinner," I reply, not making eye contact. "And I'm not good with babies."

"Why?"

"Why am I not good with babies?" I turn and stare at him. Megan smiles, a toothless smile and then sticks her fist in her mouth.

"Yeah. I mean look at her."

"She's beautiful."

Brad's phone rings in his pocket, and when he checks the caller ID, he frowns and holds the baby out to me. "Please take her, I have to take this call."

He plants Megan in my arms and walks into his office, shuts the door, and I'm left with a baby.

"How old are you, Megan?" I ask, holding her stiffly. She's watching my face, and then her own face crumples and she starts to fuss. "Oh no. Don't do that." I hold her closer to me and sway back and forth, hoping I'm doing this right. "You don't have to cry. See? It's okay."

I'm swaying and patting her back, and Megan lays her little head on my shoulder, quiet now.

Thank goodness.

With the baby on my arm, I do my best to cover

the enchiladas with foil and set them back in the oven on warm. They'll keep for a while.

Five minutes later, Brad comes out of the office, looking preoccupied.

"Sorry about that," he says and stops short when he sees me. "Well, look at you."

"I admit, she's pretty cute." I'm still swaying her back and forth, and she's tucked her little face in my neck. "Is she sleeping?"

"No, she's just hanging out." He grins and walks to us, pats Megan on the back, and then kisses me softly. "You look beautiful."

"Barefoot in the kitchen with a baby on my hip?"

"No, just beautiful," he says, then snorts out a laugh. "But that's quite the description."

"I *am* barefoot," I point out.

"But not pregnant, so there's that."

"Never," I reply, shaking my head emphatically. Megan lifts her head and looks me square in the eyes. "But you are a pretty little thing, aren't you?"

She smiles widely.

"One day, you'll get some teeth. And then, look out, because everything is delicious."

She giggles.

"That's right. All of the food is delicious."

"Speaking of food," Brad says, pulling a bottle out of a bag. He pours some formula in it, mixes it with water, and then passes it to me. "She's probably hungry."

"You feed her."

He just smiles and shakes his head no. I roll my eyes, take the bottle, and settle into his rocking recliner.

"I don't know if I'm doing this right?"

"Haven't you ever been around kids?" he asks as he watches me settle her against me and offer her the bottle, which she greedily takes, holding my hand and watching me with sleepy brown eyes.

"Not really." He passes me a rag so I can wipe up the drip on her chin. "I didn't have siblings, and I didn't babysit. I've never really felt like I'm a maternal person."

She starts to cough, choking a bit, and I immediately put the bottle down, and pull her forward, helping her airway to clear. I wipe her chin again, then settle her in to eat some more.

"Yeah, not maternal at all," he says. He's smiling when I look up at him. "I wouldn't have known how to do that."

"I'm a doctor," I remind him. "And she wasn't choking badly."

I run my fingers over her soft, fine hair and her eyes flutter closed. "She's so soft. How old is she?"

"About five months," he replies quietly, petting Sadie.

When Megan has drunk the rest of her bottle, I

settle her against my shoulder to burp her. "I think I saw this in a movie."

"You're doing great. Also, you deliver babies."

"Yes."

"You don't hold them?"

"I pull them out and hand them to their mom or a nurse, and then I go about the task of making sure Mom doesn't die."

"That's important," he says, nodding. "I had no idea that babies make you nervous."

"Well, I'm not as nervous as I was when you first arrived. Thank goodness she's not your secret baby."

"I couldn't have a secret baby in this town."

We both laugh. "True. There aren't many secrets around here."

"She's asleep," he says and drags his fingertip down her cheek. "She's a sweetie."

"I'm surprised she's not more fussy. You always hear of them crying all the time unless they're asleep. That doesn't sound fun. I always wonder, why would anyone willingly put themselves through that?"

"Is that why you don't want kids?" he asks.

I pause, thinking about it. This baby is definitely adorable. She's small, fitting against my chest perfectly, and she smells *so good*. I could bury my nose in her and stay there all day.

"I mean, she's going to wake up, right?"

"If all goes well, yes," he says, laughing again.

"And she'll cry. And probably need a lot of attention."

"She's an infant, so I'd say that's a safe assumption."

I nod, still thinking it over. "I guess that doesn't sound too bad. But I know without a doubt that I don't want to be pregnant. It goes back to me knowing too much. Most pregnancies are normal, but I see way too many that aren't. It's not something I've felt the need to experience for myself."

"Interesting," he says, sitting back on the sofa and watching me. "I guess I'd never really thought about that."

"You're a man. You don't have to worry about the changes to your body, or how well your body will even deal with being pregnant. And that's only the beginning. There can be so many different complications, diseases, disorders, and problems that it would take a month to list them all."

"And you'd worry the entire time."

"Every minute of it," I confirm. "And I know, it sounds—"

"Don't say dumb. You're not dumb, Hannah."

"Well, it sounds dumb to me," I reply with a shrug. "But it is what it is."

I pull the sleeping baby off of my chest and into my arms, so I can see her sweet face. Her lips are pursed, as if she's sucking on a nipple in her dream. "Her eyelashes are long. They're always wasted on babies and men."

"She looks like her mom," he says, just as there's a knock on the door. "Speaking of which, there they are."

"So soon?"

He tosses me a wide smile and answers the door. "She's sleeping."

"Oh, good," Dan says as they come inside. His wife, whom I immediately recognize, rushes over to check on her.

"Dr. Malone," she says with a happy smile. "What a surprise."

"Hi Alice," I reply and nod to Dan. "I didn't realize this little bundle belonged to you."

"You mean you didn't recognize her?" Dan asks with a smile.

"She was a little smaller and a lot bluer that day," I reply and smile kindly at Alice. "She's beautiful and healthy, and I'm so happy for you."

"She's here because of you," Alice says with tears in her eyes and wraps her arms around both of us, hugging us. "You saved us."

"That's the job," I say and pass the baby to her mama. "And I have to tell you, this might be the first time I've spent time with a baby that I delivered. It was fun. I had no idea this tiny baby was that Megan."

"Well, thanks to both of you for taking her so we could have an uninterrupted dinner out," Dan says, shaking Brad's hand. "It was nice."

"My pleasure," Brad says. He runs out to the garage to get the car seat base, and when they've left with the baby, he turns to me with a raised eyebrow. "I didn't know that you were the doctor who delivered her."

"I was."

"That was a shit show."

"It was." I nod, not allowed to talk freely with Brad about the medical history. "But as you can see, it all worked out."

He frowns and looks down, and then without looking me in the eyes, he just pulls me in and hugs me tightly.

"Dan would have lost both of them if it hadn't been for you, and I just want to say thank you for saving them both. Dan's a good friend."

"It's the job," I repeat, but hug him back fiercely. "And I'm happy that it all worked out for the best."

He kisses me head, breathing me in.

"Me too."

My car smells like heaven the next morning.

The aroma of coffee and donuts fills the space around me, and I want to just pull over and eat and drink it all myself.

That's not possible, but it doesn't make me want it any less.

I park in front of the police station and carry four dozen donuts and a gallon of hot coffee inside, then I run back out for the special individual coffee for Brad. As I walk back inside, Brad is approaching the desk with the donuts, where at least six other men are already loading up on sugar and caffeine.

"This one is for you," I say and hand him the cup. "The lady at *Sips* said this is what you usually order."

His eyes intently watch me as he takes a sip. "She was right. What's all this?"

"Well, I know it's a cliché, but I thought everyone might enjoy some coffee and donuts."

"You thought right," Dan says with a grin. Several other uniformed officers nod in agreement. "And these are the best donuts in town."

"I know." I reach out and snatch up a maple bar. "So good."

"Come into my office," Brad says, but I shake my head no.

"I have errands."

"Do you have two minutes?" he asks. The look on his face says he needs to talk to me, so I nod and follow him into his office, munching on my donut.

"What's up?"

He doesn't answer. Instead, he sweeps me up into a passionate kiss. He doesn't even care that I have maple glaze on my lips.

"You're sweet," he murmurs against me.

"It's the donut."

He grins and kisses me one more time, then sets me away from him. "No, it's you. You didn't have to do that for my guys."

"I know. It was fun." I smile and take another bite of my donut. "I might as well take advantage of this whole week off thing and spoil us all a little bit."

"Don't spoil them too much. They'll get soft."

"Yes, sir." I offer him a mock salute and open the office door. "I'm going to get a massage now."

"Good for you. And then?"

"I think I'll wander around downtown and look for a birthday gift for my cousin, Abby."

"Have a good day, sweetheart."

I smile and close his door behind me, waving to the guys who are smiling at me as I walk past.

I've made some friends this morning.

I'm loading up on way too much huckleberry stuff. Syrup, jam, pancake mix, even chocolate. I can't help myself. I've turned into a tourist in my own damn town.

I've wandered my way through just about every shop on Main Street in downtown Cunningham Falls. Not only did I find the cutest outfit and pair of earrings for Abby, but I found all of this huckleberry stuff, a painting for the living room of my house, *and* I might have splurged on ice cream.

Okay, I totally did.

I feel fantastic after my massage. It's a warm eighty degrees outside, perfect for roaming around without getting too hot, and it's the middle of a weekday so the tourists aren't as obnoxious as they would be on a Saturday.

Just as I'm about to walk into *Dress It Up*, I hear my name being called from across the street.

"Hannah!"

"Hey," I reply, happy to see my friend and patient, Jillian King, as she pushes her stroller across the street to join me. She has her twins with her, and her face is glowing with happiness as she joins me. "How are you?"

"I'm great," she says, panting a bit. "I took the afternoon off to take the kids to the park. It's too pretty out to waste it."

"I agree." I kneel in front of the stroller and smile at the little girl and little boy who stare back at me with curiosity. "Hello there, Sarah and Miles."

They grin and Miles offers me a high five.

"They're adorable," I say as I stand to talk to Jillian. "I can't believe how big they are."

"They'll be three soon," she says, sighing.

"And I'm going to have to come see you soon as well."

"Check up?"

She shakes her head no and gives me a happy smile. "We're expecting."

"I think at least eighty percent of the people I know are pregnant," I reply with a laugh. "Congratulations."

"What are the odds that it's twins again?" she asks nervously.

"Not high," I assure her. "Even though your husband is a twin, the odds are low."

"Thank God. I love these two, but they're a handful. Having just one infant will be a walk in the park."

"That's the way to look at it. How is Cara?"

Cara and Jillian are best friends, and each married twin brothers a few years ago. They live out at the King brothers' ranch, in separate homes, of course. The Kings own thousands of acres just west of town.

"She's great. I think she and Josh are finished having babies. Two are enough for them."

"Well, I'd love to see you all soon," I reply. "And I'll look for you on my schedule."

"Thanks," she says with a smile. "And now we're off to the park."

She walks away, in the direction of the city park down the street, and I walk into *Dress It Up* to see if I can find something new. I've shopped like a pro today, I might as well keep it going.

"Hannah," Willa says with a smile. "It's nice to see you. Can I help you find anything?"

"I'm just out shopping today," I reply. "I know I said this the other night, but I have to say it again. This store is *so pretty*."

"I know. My inner girlie girl went crazy when we were decorating. And I just can't be sorry."

"You shouldn't be. It makes me want to buy pretty things, and I would think that was the intention."

"Absolutely, and it's good to hear that it worked," she says, nodding. "Plus, when you're a single mother of a little boy, it's nice to be around girlie things sometimes."

"I'm sure. You have a son?"

"I do. He's eight." She reaches behind the glass display case that she uses for the cash register and grabs her phone, pulling up a photo. "Alexander, but we call him Alex for short."

A brunette boy with dimples and a mischievous grin stares back at me. "He's a cutie."

"He's a terror," she corrects me and tucks her phone away. "But he's eight, and he's a boy, so I'm told that being a terror is normal."

"I think so."

"So, you're dating Brad?" she asks without apology. Her chin is up, her eyes on mine, and I respect her even more. She's not trying to gossip, she's asking for information.

"We've been dating for a few weeks. Geez, more than that now, I guess."

"I've known the Hulls for a long time, and I can tell you, they don't get better than Brad."

"I'm glad you think so."

"Don't worry," she says, waving me off and straightening a shirt on a hanger. "I don't have a crush on him. If anything I feel sisterly toward him. I dated Max for a while a million years ago."

"I heard," I reply and then shrug when she raises a brow. "Small town, Willa, and I'm friends with Jenna."

"That's right." She nods and then laughs. "Max was a long time ago, but I still have a soft spot for his family. They were nice to me."

"They're nice people."

"Exactly. So, I just wanted to let you know that Brad is what you see. He's a good man, hard worker, handsome fella. And good for you for snagging him."

"Dating in this town is hard," I reply and she emphatically nods her head.

"Tell me about it. I'm either related to half the town, or I know too much about them. Or they're only here on vacation. Not to mention, I have a kid, and he comes first. Always."

"As it should be."

"A lot of men don't get that."

"A lot of men aren't worth your time then."

She stops and smiles at me. "I like you."

My phone pings with a text from Brad. *Meet me at your place at 5:00?*

"Speak of the devil," I murmur and reply with *sure.*

"Enjoy him," Willa says. "Make him loosen up a bit. He's so stuffy."

I nod and wave as I leave her store and decide to head home for a shower before Brad arrives.

Funny, he's not stuffy with me.

Hot. Sexy. Funny. But not stuffy.

CHAPTER FOURTEEN

Brad

"THIS IS...INTIMIDATING." I'm standing
next to Jenna and Max, staring up at the tree
houses that are currently under construction. They
are about thirty feet in the air, supported by metal
beams that will eventually be hidden by faux bark,
making the supports look like trees.

"Tree houses," Max murmurs and then smiles
down at Jenna. "Only you would come up with
something like this."

"It's been in my head for years," she replies
with a shrug. "And it's going to be *so cool*. If I
can get the contractor to stay on budget. This is the
second one I'll have to fire in less than a month."

"The budget is a million," Max reminds her
with a frown.

"I know. And he's almost reached it already
and we're only half way there. I would take over
and just do it myself, but these buildings are off the
ground. I need an expert for this."

Max and I share a look of concern, and then we

go off in search of the contractor together. We find him, sitting on the circular staircase in the biggest of the three houses, sipping coffee and laughing with a colleague.

"Oh, hi there, Max and Brad."

He doesn't acknowledge Jenna at all, which has me balling my hands into fists.

"We need to talk," Jenna says, but he won't make eye contact with her. "Mr. Jefferson, we need to discuss the budget."

"Oh, no need to worry," he says, but Jenna sets her hands on her hips and glares at him.

"You've almost reached my top budget and you're only half way finished with the project."

"Well, that can happen sometimes, especially when the woman in charge likes expensive things," he says and winks at me, but I just narrow my eyes at him and he loses his smug grin, clearing his throat. "Brad, I'm sure you know—"

"I don't," I interrupt. "This is Jenna's project, and you clearly don't respect that."

"The budget is the budget," Max adds. "And you don't respect that either."

"You're fired," Jenna says.

Jason Jefferson's eyes bulge and he starts to sputter. "What do you mean?"

"Fired," Jenna repeats. "Out. Canned. Done. I want you off my property in twenty minutes."

"You can't use my guys," he says nastily. "If I

go, they go."

"Fine," Jenna replies, not looking at him. "I'll find someone else."

"I'll spread rumors," he begins, but I walk forward and push my nose into his face.

"You'll what?"

"I'll spread rumors," he repeats, not backing down. "I'll tell everyone that she sleeps with the crew and her brothers try to intimidate us."

"I'm not trying," I say and lean in further, not touching him. "I'm *doing*. Despite it being a dick move, I understand that in a small town a man doesn't want to take orders from a woman. But it's the goddamn twenty-first century and this is Jenna's work site. It'll be run the way she sees fit, and she wants you gone."

"Fine," he snarls and nods to his employee. "Pack up. Let's get out of here."

"I'm an independent contractor," the young man says and turns to Jenna. "He's not my boss. I'd like to stay."

"You're welcome to stay, Bubba," she says with a smile. "Anyone else who wants to stay, and work for *me*, is welcome to do so."

Bubba nods and leaves the house, walking out to talk to the others.

"You need to leave," she says to Jason, who's seething. "And if you try to spread rumors about me or my brothers, I'll start telling the *truth* about your work ethic and ruin your business. I don't want to do that. I think this project was just too big for you, and that's okay. But it's time to call it quits."

"You're a bitch," he snarls and stomps away, gathering his tools.

"I hope he doesn't come back here to destroy what we've already done," she murmurs.

"He won't," Max says, shaking his head. "He can't chance jail time and ruining his business. He's just butt hurt."

"Who are you going to hire?" I ask her.

"I have a few calls out," she replies. "I'll get someone new right away. This project is too fun and too different. Someone will want it. I'm also going to showcase it in the Parade of Homes later this year, so they'll get exposure there as well."

"Man, Jason is a stupid son of a bitch," I reply. "But I'm glad he's gone. You don't want someone here like that."

"He wasn't always," she says and walks into the area where the kitchen will be. "He was excited in the beginning, but I meant it when I said that it got to be more than he could handle. I wish he had just been honest about it from the beginning. Male egos are fragile."

"That they are," Max says with a grin. "I can put up more money if you need it."

"I will," she says with a sigh. "Thanks to Jason. But I know that this place will pay for itself in the first three years, even with the added budget."

"I agree," Max replies with a nod. "Now that I see it in person, I know it's going to be impressive."

"Just wait," she says with an excited grin.

"Mr. Hull?" Bubba comes back into the house with a smile. "I've discussed it with the other guys, and they'd also like to stay and be a part of the project."

"It's not my project," Max reminds him. "You all need to talk to Jenna. Always."

"Of course," Bubba says and offers Jenna a chagrined smile. "Sorry about that. We'd like to stay if you'll have us."

"Let's have a quick meeting," she replies and walks outside. "Everyone who wants to stay on this project, I want you to report inside now, please."

She has her boss hat on now, and I admit, it's impressive. I'm proud of my little sister.

Once everyone has gathered inside, about eight men, she smiles at them, and then gets to business.

"I'm thankful that you'd all like to stay on the project. It's important to me, and it's going to be wonderful when its finished. But you all need to understand, *I'm the boss*. Always, every day. My brothers are investors, but that's it."

Max and I both hang in the back, our arms crossed over our chests, and watch her take the lead.

"If you have any issues with that, you're welcome to leave now."

She pauses and waits, but no one leaves.

"Great. I'll be hiring another contractor this week, and he will also be a point of contact for you. We will continue with Friday lunches being brought in, as we have been. I want you to be happy and productive."

"I don't have any issues with you at all," one of the men says. "You're fair, you're firm, and you're kind to us. Jason is a dick."

"Yes, well," Jenna says with a laugh. "I think we all agree with you. Thanks for being here, guys. We are behind schedule."

"We'll pick up the pace," someone else says. "It'll get done on time."

The rest of the men nod in agreement, and a few moments later, they go back to work and Jenna lets out a big sigh of relief.

"That could have gone very badly."

"They respect you," Max says.

"And they like you," I add. "It goes a long way."

She nods and then runs off out of the house. "Sorry guys, I remembered something I have to do in the other house."

Max and I shrug and wander out onto the large balcony that looks out onto the ski slopes, green now with summer grass and bright flowers.

"It's a good spot," Max says.

"I had my doubts, but she has something special here."

"Speaking of something special," Max begins, "tell me about Hannah."

"Touch her and I'll kill you."

He laughs and shakes his head. "No, asshole, tell me about *you* and Hannah."

"I like her." I shrug, as if it's no big deal, and lean on the railing, not meeting his eyes with mine.

"And?"

"What are you, a woman? Do you want me to tell you all about our first kiss?"

"Sure." He laughs. "You've always been the quiet one. You don't talk about personal things often."

"They're personal."

"And you're difficult."

"What do you want to hear? That I'm in love with her? That I can't imagine what life was like without her?"

"That's a start."

"It's too soon," I mutter and shake my head in frustration. "It's been less than two months."

"So?" I jerk my gaze to his. "Who gives a fuck about how much time has passed? You're not strangers, and you've spent enough time together to know how you feel about her."

"She's amazing," I reply simply. "She has the next few days off of work, and I'd like to do something special for her."

"Can you take some time off work?" Max asks.

"Yeah, I have plenty of paid time off coming."

"I have an idea," he says. "Take her to my condo in Laguna Beach. Use the plane."

"Impress her," I reply, not hating the idea.

"Treat her," he counters. "Go live it up a little."

"I don't like taking advantage of you."

"Jesus Christ," he mutters and pushes his hand through his hair. "I understand that you don't want me to pay off your house. But for fucksake, Brad, I own these things out right, and I'm not using them. *You* should use them. Take your girl for a romantic weekend at the beach."

"Okay."

He looks up, his eyes wide with surprise. "Yeah?"

"Yeah, that would be fun. Thank you."

Max lets out a sigh. "I thought you'd never agree to it."

"I'm proud of you," I say and turn to face him. "I couldn't be more proud. You've made more money than you can ever spend on your own, and you did it with grit and determination. You're smart. Of course I'm proud of you. But those things are *yours*, not mine. I like making my own way."

"I know, and I respect that. But using some of the things I've made or bought isn't freeloading. I *want* to share all of this with my family. Otherwise, what's the fucking point?"

I blink, not thinking of it this way before. "Thanks for that."

"You're welcome. Now go soak up some beach time with Hannah. Have vacation sex. Laugh. I think you both could use it."

"That's the truth. I need to make arrangements at work, but is the jet available this afternoon?"

"It's ready when you are."

"Can you keep Sadie?"

"Of course. That dog loves me more than she does you."

"Whatever."

"I'll call down to the condo and tell them you're coming. Everything will be ready for you."

"I owe you."

"No. You don't. That's the whole point."

Work is squared away. I was surprised by how easily they all agreed to look after things for me while I'm gone.

I guess it's been a minute since I took a vacation.

Sadie is safely with Max, my house is locked up tight, and I've called the airport. The plane is ready.

Max has owned it for a few years, but I've only ridden in it once before. It feels odd. Indulgent. Ridiculous, honestly. I mean, why would I need to ride in a private plane?

But Hannah will get a kick out of it. I've seen photos of Max's condo in southern California.

We'll both get a kick out of that.

I haven't been excited for a trip like this in a long time.

I pull up to Hannah's house and see her car parked in the drive. She's at her computer when I walk inside, her gorgeous red hair piled on her head, and she's only wearing a tank top and panties, her legs pulled up under her in the chair.

She's a fucking wet dream.

But we don't have time for me to live out the dream right now.

"Hi, sweetheart."

She smiles and looks up, offering her lips for a kiss, which I gladly accept. I sink into her, kissing her much more deeply than I'd planned, and I have to tear myself away from her if we're going to leave the house today.

"I have a surprise for you."

"Really?" Her smile widens. "Flowers?"

"Better."

"Coffee?"

"Better."

She lifts a brow. "Better than coffee?"

"Oh yeah. I want you to pack a bag."

She frowns now and stands up out of the chair, and my semi-hard on is now at full alert.

"Where are we going?"

"It's a surprise. You'll also need pants."

"Will I need a passport?"

"Not this time." I grin and cup her cheek, unable to keep myself from touching her. "We're just going away for a few days."

"Warm or cold climate?"

"Why?"

"I need to know what to pack, Chief Sexypants."

I cringe at the horrible nickname. "Warm. Think beach."

"Oh, the beach!" She claps her hands and jogs to her closet. "How fun. I'll take lots of flip flops, a few bathing suits." She pokes her head around the doorjamb, her hair falling in her eyes. "Will we need to dress up for anything?"

"Possibly."

She narrows her eyes and then shrugs. "Okay. I'll pack a sundress. Shorts. Tanks. Maybe a sweater in case it's cold in the evenings."

"We're only going for a few days," I remind her as she rushes past me to the bathroom.

"I know, but you just never know what I might need. All the makeup, hair stuff." She gathers all the girl products in the world into her arms and tosses them into her suitcase, then proceeds to organize everything just so. "Okay, I think I have everything. Do I need to do my hair and makeup for the plane?"

"No." I take her shoulders in my hands and turn her to me. "You look beautiful just like this."

"I'm a mess."

"I don't think so."

"And I'm not wearing pants."

"That doesn't bother me either."

She chuckles and kisses my chin. "When do we have to leave?"

"In about thirty minutes."

Her eyes go wide. "Brad! We won't make the plane in time!" She rushes to pull on shorts, slips into sandals, and zips her suitcase closed. "We have to hurry."

CHAPTER FIFTEEN

Hannah

I DON'T KNOW WHY he's so calm. We have *minutes* to get to the gate in time. There's no way they'll let us through security now.

Is this what I'm destined to deal with all the time if I stay with him forever? Because I have to be honest, I can't do that. I'm way too organized for that. I get to the airport *at least* an hour before the flight takes off.

I mean, who shows up with only a few minutes to spare?

"It's going to be fine," Brad says with a smile as he turns toward the airport.

"Do you want to just drop me off and I'll run in and check us in?"

"No."

I stare at him and then shake my head, completely knotted up inside. But, I should calm down. This is *his* show, and if the plane leaves without us, that's not my fault.

Yeah. That's it.

Rather than pull into the parking lot, he takes a turn on what looks like an employees' road that winds behind the airport, back where the planes are parked.

"We're going to get in trouble," I mutter, but he just chuckles next to me. "Who *are* you? You're acting very weird."

"Relax. I know that's not easy for you, but I've got this. We're not getting in trouble."

I sigh, not believing him in the least, but decide to take both our advice. What's the worst that will happen? We won't go on this trip?

Hell, an hour ago I didn't even know there was a trip.

He turns away from the commercial airliners and drives over to a smaller plane that has the main door open, the stairs pushed against it like it's waiting for passengers.

"This is our ride," he says casually and parks about ten yards from the plane.

"This?"

"Yes, ma'am." He winks before getting out of his truck, talks to a member of the ground crew, and opens my door for me. "Your carriage awaits."

"We're taking a *private* plane?"

"We are."

I hop out of his truck and stare at the gleaming white and black jet, completely shocked.

"Wow."

"Hi, Chief." A man steps out of the plane and shakes Brad's hand. "We're ready when you are, sir."

"Great, thanks. We're ready any time. Hannah, this is Jeremy. He's the pilot today."

"It's a great day for a flight. Smooth sailing the whole way." He smiles and walks back inside the plane and disappears.

"I requested that we not have a flight attendant today," he says with a smile and leads me inside the jet. It's bigger than I thought it would be. There are at least a dozen plush leather seats, all comfortable recliners that swivel. "There's a bathroom in the back, and there's a galley with snacks and drinks if you want anything."

"I'm fine," I reply, completely shocked. "This is gorgeous. How did you manage this?"

"It's Max's plane," he says and helps me fasten my seatbelt. The pilot quickly comes back to go over safety features and introduce us to the co-pilot, and then he disappears behind the door leading to the cockpit and I hear the engines start. "We're using all of his fun toys over the next few days."

"That's pretty cool." The seat feels like a big hug, wrapping around my body and cradling me. "This might be the most comfortable airplane seat I've ever been in."

"I'm glad you like it."

"What's not to like? It's a super fancy treat. Max seems nice."

"I like him," Brad replies with a shrug. "He's generous, and he hasn't let all the money go to his head."

"That's good." I nod and watch as Brad takes a seat across from me, swivels to face me, and clicks his own seatbelt closed. He crosses one ankle over the opposite knee and rubs his fingers over his mouth, watching me with hot green eyes.

"What's wrong?"

"There's no fucking loveseat or couch on this plane," he says immediately. "As soon as we're airborne, I'm pulling you into my lap."

I laugh, but electricity is zinging through me at the intensity of his voice. "I guess I've been warned."

He doesn't reply, and we're quiet as the plane picks up speed down the runway and takes off. I glance outside, surprised that the plane ride isn't bumpier as it climbs away from the green trees and blue lakes below into the sky.

"A smaller plane usually means more turbulence," I comment and turn to find him still watching me.

"This plane is pretty steady."

I nod and squeeze my legs closed, completely taken off guard at the sexual tension in the air. If I thought it was there earlier at my house, it's nothing like right now.

I'm going to have sex in an airplane.

That's new.

We sit, staring at each other, until there's a ding over the speakers that signals we're at cruising altitude and we're safe to move about.

Within seconds, Brad is out of his seat and next to me, unclipping my seatbelt and lifting me into his arms.

My hands dive into his hair as his lips find mine, and it's like we're starved for each other, like we haven't been together in ages rather than just this morning.

Rather than sit with me in his lap, Brad quickly strips us both out of our clothes, and guides me down to sit in my seat, scooted forward so my ass is at the very edge of the chair.

The next thing I know, he pushes my legs up, spreads them wide, and buries his face in my core, making me bite my lip to keep from crying out.

I don't need to alert the pilots to the show happening twenty feet behind them.

"You're so damn sweet," he growls, watching me as he licks and nibbles, then pulls my lips into his mouth and makes a pulsing motion, succeeding in puckering my nipples.

I'm quite sure I'm going to have a bloody lip by the time this is over.

And I couldn't care less.

"You can make noise," he says.

"No way." I have to grip the arms of the chair

for dear life, not worried in the least that I might pierce the leather with my nails. "They can hear."

"No, they can't." He grins and pushes a finger inside me, watching me almost leisurely. "They have headsets on to talk to air traffic control. They're in their own world."

I gasp when he pushes a second finger inside and makes a *come here* motion, making me quiver and see stars all at once.

"Oh God."

"That's right."

"I can't even."

"Oh yes. You can." He lowers his mouth to my clit, and that's it. I explode into a million pieces. Without missing a beat, he wraps his arms around my back and picks me up, settling in the seat and me on top of him, straddling his hips.

I lower myself onto him, and when he's buried as far as he can go, I lean in and kiss his mouth, loving the smell and taste of me on his lips.

"You make me crazy," I whisper.

"Not nearly as crazy as you make me," he counters, gripping my ass and urging me to move up and down in a long, quick motion. "I couldn't wait to get airborne so I could have my way with you."

"I have to admit, this is a first."

He fists his hand in my hair and pulls me down to kiss him. "You make me want things I never have before, Hannah."

"Like what?"

I bear down and squeeze, making him clench his teeth.

"This. Sex where someone could hear."

"You said they *can't* hear."

He grins. "Well, they probably can't."

I pause, momentarily mortified, and then throw caution to the wind and move faster, bearing down harder.

"Trying to make me come?"

"Hell, yes," I reply and bite his neck. "And I want you to be loud."

His fingertips dig into my hips and every muscle in his body tightens as I continue to nibble and bite. And when I sink my fingers into his hair again, he cries out and comes apart, leaving me with a very satisfied smile.

"You look like the cat that ate the canary."

"Or the girl who made you come," I counter. "I'll have bruises on my ass later."

He frowns. "I'm sorry."

"Don't ever apologize for that," I reply as I stand and walk, naked, to the back of the plane. Once I've cleaned up, I return to find Brad already dressed, my clothes laid out on the chair we just had wild plane sex on.

I watch him as I pull on my clothes, fluff my

hair, and sit opposite him, the way we started this trip.

"Would you like something to drink?" he asks casually, his voice calm.

"You sure do switch gears quickly."

"I always want you, Hannah. I could take you again right now. But we'll take a break. In the meantime, I'm thirsty."

"Me too." I smile gratefully, my nipples puckered all over again. "A Coke would be great."

"Done." He stands to go fetch our drinks, but pauses to lean in and kiss me thoroughly. "I'm going to fuck you frequently over the next few days."

"Thank God."

"Jesus." I drop my handbag on the table by the doorway of the condo and stop to stare straight ahead. It's all beautiful, but the view is already my favorite part.

And I'm barely inside.

We're on the top floor of an owners' building of this resort on the beach in southern California. Laguna Beach, to be exact. I've never been any farther west than Montana, and never to an ocean.

This is just spectacular.

"The penthouse has three bedrooms," Brad begins as he carries the luggage into a bedroom, and then returns to look at me, then the view, and back at me again. "Hannah?"

"Yeah?"

"Are you okay?"

The ocean is bright blue, and disappears into a sky just as blue as the water. There are palm trees and brown sand and a pool with a sunshine embedded in the tile below us.

I turn to stare at Brad, and then launch myself into his arms, kissing him crazy.

"I take it that's a yes," he says with a smile when I pull back.

"I've never seen anything like this."

"Is this your first time to the ocean?"

I nod and when he sets me on my feet, I make a beeline for the sliding glass doors that lead out to a covered balcony, big enough for a dining table that seats six, a gas fire pit and a sectional sofa.

"This is *amazing*."

"Max chose well when he bought this place," Brad replies as he joins me at the railing. "He says it's a good investment, and while I'm sure that's true, he also spends quite a bit of time here."

"Why would he ever go home to Montana?"

"Have you seen his house there?"

I shake my head no and he grins.

"It may not have this view, but it's pretty great as well. Come on, I want to show you the condo and then we can do whatever you want."

He takes my hand and leads me inside, pointing out five bathrooms, three of which are attached to bedrooms, a formal living space, and a dining room off of a gleaming white gourmet kitchen.

When he takes me into the master bedroom and shows me the adjoining bath and closet, all I can do is laugh.

"You've got to be kidding me. This is a *vacation* home?"

"I know, it's crazy."

"Brad, this closet is my dream closet."

I turn in a circle, taking it in. It must be two hundred square feet, with floor to ceiling shelving and built in dressers. There's a vanity area, and a chandelier hanging from the ceiling over an island with more drawer space.

"It's mostly empty," I murmur.

"Max is single," Brad reminds me. "And he's here about six months out of the year."

"A woman should be using this closet. I need to set him up with someone."

He laughs and tucks my hair behind my ear. "He does fine by himself. We'll take the smaller master suite on the other side of the condo. It also has a sweet bathroom and an ocean view. I'm not going to have sex in my brother's bed."

"Ew. No." I laugh and follow him back to the living room. "This is just amazing. Thank you for bringing me here."

"There was no way you'd survive a whole

week off at home," he says with a laugh.

"I've taken weeks off before."

"Not unplanned," he points out and I have to nod in agreement. "This way, you're really on vacation. No need to feel guilty for being lazy or indulgent."

"You're good to me."

He simply smiles and kisses my forehead. "What would you like to do first?"

"I'm putting my bathing suit on, grabbing my iPad, and parking my ass by the pool to read a book."

"Excellent," he says with a smile. "Let's do it."

"I can't believe I fell asleep by the pool," I grumble later that evening at dinner. It's a bit early, but I woke up starving, so Brad took me back to the condo to change clothes so we could eat at one of the resort restaurants. Our table is by the window so I can look out at the water. "Thanks for pulling the umbrella over me."

"I know you say you tan, but that much sun can't be good for a redhead." He spreads some butter on a piece of bread and passes it to me. "Here. Eat."

"Yes, sir." I take a bite and close my eyes in happiness. "Oh, it's fresh out of the oven."

"Keep making that face," he says quietly.

My eyes fly up to his in confusion.

"I'm already hard," he says and takes a bite of his own bread. "You're about three seconds from me carrying you out of here."

I smirk and take another bite. We ordered pasta, and I can't wait. If it's half as good as this bread, I'll be in heaven.

"Did I miss anything good during my nap?"

"No," he replies with a smile. "And you looked sexy as hell with your sunglasses on, your iPad resting on your chest."

"What did you do?"

"I got a little work done. I took a call and sent an email on my phone."

Our food is delivered, smelling absolutely delicious. I take a bite and decide on the spot that I want to live here all the time.

"This is so good."

"Delicious," he agrees, but I shake my head no.

"All of it. The plane, the condo, the ocean. Being here and doing it all with you. It's amazing. And I know that you didn't have to take time from work, and that doing so at the last minute was probably stressful, so thank you. I won't complain or say you shouldn't have because frankly, it's all too fantastic. I'm so happy that you did. But I know it wasn't easy."

"I haven't taken time away in a long time myself," he admits. "Too long, honestly. My crew was happy to see me go, and I know they have everything handled. I just had a few things to wrap up, and you napping gave me the opportunity to do that. But you're welcome. It was a spur of the moment idea. I'd been up on the mountain at the tree house project with Jenna and Max, and after our meeting, I was talking about you with Max."

"What were you saying?" I smile innocently, bat my eyelashes, and take a sip of my water.

"That's classified," he says. "But then it occurred to me that Max is always offering the plane and condo to Jenna and me and we never take him up on it. You have time off, and it's not hard for me to take off for a couple of days. So here we are."

"Was Max surprised?"

"Oh yeah. But pleasantly so. I mentioned earlier that he's generous. It's true, he is. He's paid for our parents' winter place, so they didn't have to sell the Cunningham Falls house to pay for it. Now they have both."

"That's awesome."

"He's funding the tree house project, but that'll pay him back within a couple of years. Jenna's vision for it is amazing. She won't have any issue with drawing in tourists."

"She's so smart."

He nods. "So while my brother is a pain in the ass a lot, he's also a good man. And he's generous with his family."

"He's a pain in the ass because he's your brother."

"Of course."

I laugh and sit back, finished with my dinner. "This was *so good*."

"I've heard the dessert menu in this place is ridiculous."

"Well, we're going to have to sit here for a minute so I can hold it. Because I'm totally getting some."

He grins and then looks up when the waiter approaches.

"I have binoculars for you," he says and sets them on the table. "There seems to be some whale activity."

He points outside, and I immediately reach for the binoculars, in complete awe of the enormous humpback whales that are jumping out of the water.

"Seems it's dinner time for them, too," Brad says.

"Is that what they're doing?"

"I don't know, it sounded good."

I pass him the binoculars so he can see them too. He watches for a moment, then hands them back to me, and I watch while he settles the check with the waiter.

"I have an idea," Brad says. "Let's go down and walk on the beach for a while, let our dinner settle, and watch the whales. We can always come back later for dessert."

"You're a smart man, Chief Sexypants."

He rolls his eyes and stands, holding his hand out for mine.

"Are you ever going to stop calling me that?"

"Nope."

CHAPTER SIXTEEN

Hannah

"**I HOPE I DON'T** step on a jellyfish."

We're on the sand, walking down to the water. I have the binoculars hanging around my neck for whale watching, we stepped out of our shoes at the beach entrance, and we're both in shorts, so there's no need to roll our pants legs.

"I'll keep an eye out for any rogue jellyfish," he says. He's holding my hand, our fingers linked. The sun is just starting to set on the horizon.

"I read somewhere that when they sting you, it hurts really bad and the only way to take the sting away is to pee on it."

"Well, that's a delightful thought," he says. "I'm not really into that sort of thing."

I push his arm, making him splash in the water. "I'm not either, perv."

"I will defend you against all jellyfish and the threat of pee."

"And they say chivalry is dead."

He stops in front of me, his back to me. "Hop on."

"I'm not gonna pass that up." I hop onto his back and he catches me around the knees. I wrap my arms around his shoulders and lean in to kiss his ear. "This is nice."

He doesn't say anything for a while as he carries me down the beach. I'm watching intently for whales and laughing at seagulls who have flown over to see what we're up to, and to see if we have a hand out.

He finally sets me down, and I plant my feet in the sand, ready for the water to wash over them.

"Oh, it's like bath water."

"It's warm in the summer," he agrees and watches me with happy eyes. "You look beautiful like this."

"Like what?"

"Happy. Playful."

I stop and tip my head back, take a deep breath and smile. "I feel happy. And you were right, I've been able to relax, and that's a huge gift."

"And it's only day one," he reminds me.

"That's right." We're walking further down the beach. The sky is a riot of orange, blue, and purple. The sand is getting rockier, so we turn back toward the resort. "We walked further than I thought."

"It's easy to do on the beach."

"Have you been here often?"

"I've actually never visited this resort before, but I love the ocean. When I was a kid, my parents would bring us to the Oregon coast every summer. It's colder up there, but still fun."

"I love it. I didn't know what I was missing." I glance up at the resort, all lit up in the twilight. "It's beautiful."

"And quieter than I expected. I thought it would be flooded with tourists."

"It's mid-week. Maybe that has something to do with it." He nods, and I keep rambling. "You know what else I'm enjoying?"

"What's that?"

"We don't have to share each other. Neither of us is in danger of being called in to work, and we're not putting in odd hours. I get to spend a block of time with you, uninterrupted. That might be the best vacation of all."

"We should do it often. Just schedule it and make it happen."

"I would do that." I actually *love* that idea.

"Or, better yet, you should just move in with me."

I trip on my own feet, surprised at the suggestion, and Brad catches me before I fall on my face.

"Easy. Are you okay?"

"I'm fine."

Holy shit! I'm not fine. He just asked me to move in with him as casually as asking me to go to the movies.

We've never said the L word.

I've almost said it once or twice, but that's not the same as saying it. Not even close. How can he ask me to live with him if he doesn't love me?

"What do you think?"

"About what?"

Okay, that was lame. But I don't know what to say.

"Moving in with me." He smiles down at me and tucks a strand of hair behind my ear.

"Well, I guess I'll have to think about it."

"Makes sense," he says with a nod, and then he completely drops the subject. So now I don't know if he regrets mentioning it, or if it's really that casual of a thing for him.

And of course I'm going to spend forever over-thinking it. I wish I had my phone on me; I'd text Abby.

I'll text her when we get back. She'll know what to say.

"You're suddenly quiet," he says.

"I think I'm just tired," I lie, feeling guilty about it. I'm all pumped up with adrenaline now. "It's been a long day."

"So should we skip dessert and go up to the condo?"

"I think that's a good idea."

He nods and leads me up to our condo, and once inside, I make a beeline for the bathroom. I lock the door and stand in front of the mirror, staring at myself.

I look not a little scared.

Because I am.

"He just asked you to move in with him and you clammed up," I whisper to myself and shake my head in disgust. What does that mean? That maybe I don't love him? That I should break up with him?

I frown and shake my head, dismissing that idea. There's no need to be rash.

"Hannah?"

"Just a minute."

I take a deep breath, push my fingers through my hair, and glare at my reflection in the mirror.

Pull it together.

I open the door to find Brad leaning against the wall, waiting for me.

"There are other bathrooms," I point out and walk into the living room with Brad on my heels.

"What's going on?"

"With whom?"

"With you." He grabs my arm to stop me from pacing. "Talk to me. I can hear the wheels turning in that gorgeous head of yours."

"You threw me," I reply and pull out of his

grasp. "How can you just toss those words out so casually, like it's nothing? It's not nothing, Brad. It's not a little thing."

"Moving in with me?"

"Yes." I roll my eyes and pace away from him. "*You should move in with me.* Like you're asking me to hike in the park."

"I may not be good at words, Hannah, but you're right. It's not a little thing. It's the biggest thing in my life." My eyes fly to his bright ones. His jaw is tight, his hands fisted. "I hate that I only get to see you a few times a week because of the responsibility of our jobs. I don't want to see you when we can both squeeze it in."

"So, it would be convenient then."

"Yes. No. Fucking hell." He shoves his hands through his hair and stomps away from me and then back again. "You're infuriating, you know that?"

"Back at you."

"I love you, goddamn it." He grips my shoulders and pulls me closer to him. "I don't want to live without you. I can't focus on anything *but* you, Hannah. When I'm not with you, I'm thinking about you. I want you to move in with me so I can see you more, spend more time with you, sleep next to you every night."

"Brad."

But he doesn't let me finish. He scoops me up and hauls me into the bedroom, lifts my sundress over my head and tosses it carelessly on the floor, then guides me onto the bed. He shimmies out of his clothes and covers me completely.

"You always make me feels so small when I'm under you."

"You are small," he murmurs and kisses my cheek. "But so fucking strong. Brave. Funny." He kisses down my neck to my breast and plucks my nipple in his teeth. "Sweet."

"Oh my."

"Listen to me."

"I'm listening."

I glance down to find him smiling up at me. "I love the hell out of you, sweetheart."

I swallow hard and let my head fall back, staring at the ceiling.

Don't cry. That would be so damn embarrassing.

"Look at me."

"You're bossy." But I do as he says. He looks mighty pleased with himself.

"This." His hand covers my core. "You." He kisses my navel and then higher on my breast bone. "Are mine."

I cock a brow and watch as he lays open-mouthed kisses all over my torso, leaving heat and electricity in his wake.

"That's right," he continues, not waiting for me to respond. "Your body and your heart belong to me, Hannah."

"Awfully sure of yourself, Chief Se—"

"Now isn't the time to be funny," he growls and covers me again, his face even with mine. "I'm serious, Hannah. You're mine, goddamn it, and I want you with me."

"If I'm yours, you're mine too. It works both ways."

He frowns as if he's confused. "Of course. Haven't you heard what I'm saying to you?"

"Yes. You're claiming me, and telling me, but you haven't said anything about being mine, and that's the only way this is going to work."

"Baby, of course I'm yours. I told you, I don't see anything *but* you." His fingers gently glide down my cheeks as he sinks inside me, making me gasp in pleasure. "I'm yours completely. *That's* why I want you to move in with me. Everything I am, and all that I have belongs to you."

"I just want you," I whisper and moan when he begins to move in earnest. "Because I love you too. I've wanted to say it for a while, but I thought it might be too soon."

"If it's how you feel, it's not too soon."

I smile and lift up to kiss him. "You're not so bad with words, you know."

He tips his forehead against mine and moves in a steady, even rhythm. He's not fucking me now. He's making love to me more beautifully than ever before.

He's strong and masculine and brave. And with me he's gentle and sweet. I trust him. I enjoy him.

I love him.

"So what do you say? Are you going to move in with me?"

"Of course."

He grins. "You had me worried there for a minute."

I cup his face gently. "I'm yours, remember? No need to worry."

"You slept late," I say the next morning as Brad comes stumbling out onto the deck. He's rubbing the sleep from his eyes. "Do you want coffee?"

"Please." He drops onto the couch next to me and curls into me, snuggling closely.

"I can't pour the coffee with you on me."

"Coffee after this."

I smile and run my fingers through his hair the way he likes. We were up most of the night, making plans and just talking. One thing about Brad and me is we never run out of things to talk about.

The sun is up and the world is awake, and I didn't want to miss it.

"How long have you been up?" he asks.

"About an hour. I ordered room service, and I've been out here soaking in the ocean."

"I'm glad you love it here," he says and sits up. I reach over and pour him a cup of coffee, fix it up the way he likes, and pass it to him.

"You're usually the one making me coffee. This is kind of nice."

"I don't remember the last time I slept this late."

"You needed it." I set my iPad aside and take a bite of my bagel with cream cheese. "Do you feel rested?"

"Yeah. And ready to get busy making plans."

"For today?"

"For when we get home and we move you into my place."

I laugh. "We have plenty of time for that. You don't have to spend our vacation worrying about it."

"I want it done ASAP. What are you going to do with your house? I assume you own it?"

"I'll rent it out for a while. It's a great investment, and I don't see a reason to sell it right away."

"Are you keeping it as a way out if things don't work out for us?"

I frown and take another bite of my bagel. "I don't like to think that way, Brad. I don't think that things will go badly. But I'd be a fool if I didn't have a back up plan."

He watches me for a moment, his eyes cool.

"Come on, if it were Jenna, would you suggest she sell her house tomorrow and go live happily ever after with some guy?"

"If that's what she wants." I give him the *whatever* look and he shrugs. "Okay, no. I'd recommend she keep her house and that she be careful. But I would wish her well if the guy was as fantastic as I am."

I laugh and scoot into his lap. "Well, that goes without saying. And I'm not bullshitting about the investment thing. Owning property in our little resort town is lucrative."

"You're right. Rent it out, sell it, hell, do whatever you want with it. It's yours, after all." He pulls his phone out of his shorts pocket and opens the messages. "I'm going to text a few guys I know to get some movers reserved. I figure with your schedule, you'll need help with packing and stuff."

"I hadn't thought of that, but it's a good idea. I'll want to be on hand when they're in my house, though."

"We'll both be there." He's typing out quick messages, and my own phone pings with a text.

Where the fuck are you?

"Oops. I forgot to tell Drake that I was leaving town."

I bite my lip and type out a quick response and attach a photo of Brad and me at the pool yesterday.

"Is he angry?"

"Probably worried," I reply. "He'll be shocked when I tell him I'm moving in with you."

"Why?"

"Because I've always said that I probably won't ever do the commitment thing. Who wants to deal with a doctor for a girlfriend?"

"I don't seem to mind it," he replies, his attention still on his phone.

"You know, it's impressive that you're able to text and still hold a conversation with me at the same time."

"I'm a man of many talents."

I grin and there's a response from Drake.

You scared me. We're supposed to let each other know when we go out of town.

"See? He's just worried."

I know. I'm sorry. It happened really fast! It was a surprise from Brad. But all is well and I'll tell you all about it when I get home.

"I have movers coming next Tuesday."

"That's in four days."

His eyes find mine. "Is that a problem?"

I just laugh and shake my head. "When you decide you want something, you don't waste any time."

"Not when it comes to you, sweetheart. What do you want to do today?"

"I want to walk on the beach again. Or better yet, go for a run on the beach. And then I want to be lazy at the pool for the rest of the day."

"We can do those things." He leans in and kisses me sweetly. "Thank you."

"For what?"

"For all of it."

CHAPTER SEVENTEEN

Hannah

"I'VE HARDLY SEEN YOU since you got home," Grace says a week later. We're packing up my house, or what's left after all of my important personal things were already taken over to Brad's just a few days ago.

"I know, it's been a whirlwind." I sit back on my heels and push my messy hair out of my face, then decide *fuck it* and tie it up on my head. "I went back to work, and we started moving my stuff all around the same time, so we've been busy *and* exhausted."

"I can't believe you took the plunge," Drake says, who's busy stacking boxes. "You're sure it's what you want?"

"Yes." I stick my tongue out at him. "I'm happy and in love. Just be happy for me."

"I'm happy for you. I just want to make sure you weren't pressured into anything. It feels sudden."

I shake my head and go back to stacking books

in boxes. "It's not sudden. We've been dating for a few months, and we know that we love each other, so why not live together? You know how crazy our hours are, and Brad's can be just as hectic. We want to be able to spend as much of our downtime together as possible."

"I think that makes sense," Grace says with a shrug. "Although, I'm not a good judge of that sort of thing because I moved in with Jacob after knowing him for a week."

"*That's* fast," I say and look at Drake as if to say, *see?* "And even though it was fast, it worked out wonderfully for you."

"It did," she says with a happy smile. "And I have no doubt that this is going to work out for you and Brad. I can see the way you smile when he walks into a room. It's adorable."

"Adorable," Drake agrees, propping his hands on his hips.

"Yes, I can see that you're happy for me," I reply.

"I'm cautious," he replies grimly. "Because I love you and I *know* you. I'm protective."

"Like a pesky brother."

"Exactly," he says with a smile. "Someone needs to be. And I do want the best for you. I want you happy and in love and all that happy crap."

"He's so romantic," Grace says.

"And I want you to be smart," he continues

without acknowledging Grace. "Because while falling in love is fun, it's also sometimes blinding."

"I'm not blind," I reply, not angry with Drake in the least. "Honestly, I'm not. He's a human being, and he's not perfect. But he's pretty wonderful anyway, and he loves me. I love him, too. That's a good reason to want to live together."

"Okay then," Drake replies with a nod. "You know I support you. Always. But I'm also going to be the pesky brother who watches over you."

"How sweet." I pat his cheek, and then give it a little squeeze, making him cringe. "You're the best brother a girl could have."

He rolls his eyes and gets back to work packing boxes.

"Why do I have so much crap? I've only lived in this house for like four and a half years."

"That's what we do," Grace says. "We gather things. And then they fill up our house and we wonder why we have so much of it."

"I haven't cracked these books open in years."

"And yet," Drake says, "you're piling them in boxes and I'm hauling them around."

"I mean, your muscles are impressive when you lift heavy things," I say helpfully, but he just glowers at me. "Also, you love me."

"That's why," he says, shaking his head.

"So, you and Brad had a romantic time at the beach?" Grace asks with a grin. "Tell us everything."

"It was *so beautiful,* you guys. You both should go sometime. The resort is just stellar, with amazing food and views. I haven't been that relaxed in... hell, I don't remember the last time I was that relaxed."

"That's awesome." Grace smiles as she rubs her little belly. "I told Jacob that I want to go sometime, and he said he'd make it happen. What a great place to spend some of this pregnancy, when I'm big and uncomfortable."

"You should do that," I reply with a nod. "You can lay by the pool with a book and just relax. It would be perfect. But I don't want you to fly after you hit the eight-month mark."

"Yes, Dr. Malone," she says with a smile. "And speaking of me being pregnant, Jacob has also said that he's going to wrap me from head to toe in bubble wrap so I'm sure not to hurt me or the baby."

"You'll be fine," I reply and then cock my head to the side, thinking. "Actually, we should just put you in a bubble all the time."

"Probably," she says. "Drake, this box is full."

"So, I'm basically just the slave around here today," he grumbles.

"You're the brawn of our operation," I agree. "You like feeling needed and you know it."

"Maybe." He tapes Grace's box shut and then carries it to the growing pile against the wall. "So what did you decide to do with all of this?"

258 | KRISTEN PROBY

"Well, not all of it will fit in Brad's house. So, I took over what's most important to me already. Clothes, toiletries, electronics. You know, all that stuff. Now we're packing up the rest of my personal things to go to storage until I have time to sift through it all and decide what to do."

"What about the furniture? It's practically brand new," Grace says.

"Well, I was talking to Jenna the other day, and she suggested rather than making this place a monthly rental, I make it a vacation rental. I hadn't thought of it before, but I looked at comps in the area for what the income potential could be, and it just made sense. So I'm going to move out the personal stuff and spruce up what's already here and rent it out to tourists."

"Jenna's smart," Grace says. "That's a great idea. And around here the earning potential has to be fantastic."

"Yeah, and the potential for asshole tourists is fantastic too," Drake says, scowling. "They'll wreck the place."

"Not all of them," I say. "What the hell is wrong with you today? You're so moody."

"I'm always moody."

"You're particularly sunshiny today," Grace says, batting her eyelashes innocently.

"There's nothing wrong with me," he says. "But if I'd known I was going to be moving all of these damn boxes, I wouldn't have gone to the gym this morning."

"You don't have to be here," I remind him. "I have a dolly that I can use to move stuff around."

"I don't want either of you moving this stuff," he says and I just cock a brow, watching him.

"You get this way when you haven't gotten laid in a while," I say, tapping my lips with my finger. "Is that it?"

"To be fair, I get testy when I haven't gotten laid in a while," Grace adds, making me smile. I nod in agreement, and Drake rolls his eyes. He's the king of the eye-roll today.

"There's absolutely nothing wrong."

"Bullshit," I reply. "I've known you for a dozen years, and there's something bugging you."

"I lost a patient last night." He leans against the wall and wipes the sweat from his brow. "It was a fluke, and it was during surgery. Routine gall bladder removal. It shouldn't have happened."

"I'm sorry." I stand and walk to him, wrap my arms around his waist and hug him close. This is the hardest part about what we do because eventually we're faced with the reality that we're human, and we can't save everyone. "I'm very sorry."

"I'll be okay," he says and squeezes me tightly. "And I'm sorry I'm an asshole."

"It's okay." I pull back with a smile. "You're only an asshole part of the time."

His lips twitch just as the doorbell rings. I open

the door and freeze. There are two Montana Highway Patrol officers standing on my porch.

"Brad." I reach blindly for Drake's hand. If something's happened to Brad, I don't know what I'll do. I can't lose him. I just found him. "Please tell me it's not Brad."

"No, ma'am."

I sigh in relief, adrenaline coursing through my body. "Thank God."

"I'm patrolman Peterson, and this is my partner, patrolman James. Can we please come inside?"

"Sure." I step back and allow them in. "I'm moving, so the place is a mess."

"We won't be long. You'll want to sit down."

My eyes fly to both Grace and Drake, who are both watching the officers with suspicion. Grace has her phone gripped in her hand.

"What's this about?"

Both men, in their forties with grim faces, look at each other. Patrolman Peterson says, "Would you rather we talk in private?"

"No, I'd rather you tell me what's going on."

He nods and takes a deep breath. "I'm sorry to inform you that Randall Malone was killed yesterday morning in a motor vehicle accident just outside of Billings, Montana."

"What?" Suddenly both Drake and Grace are flanking me, each holding one of my hands, and the blood is rushing in my ears. "That can't be possible. He doesn't live in Montana."

"No, ma'am. But he was driving through Montana, for what purpose we can't be sure."

"But I live in Cunningham Falls," I whisper and close my eyes. "That asshole was coming here."

"He was in a multiple vehicle accident yesterday," he repeats, "and he was the only fatality."

"Well, at least there's that." Drake squeezes my hand and I just shake my head. "Thanks for letting me know."

"That's not all," he continues. "It seems you're the only surviving relative of your father's, so we need to know where you want the body to be transported to."

"Excuse me?" I scowl and pull my hands free so I can fist them. "I *don't* want him."

"Well, you can choose to not claim him," the patrolman says. "But in that case—"

"Can she think about it?" Grace asks, interrupting him. "Is there a number she can call you at once she's had the chance to think it all through and take it in. This is a lot of information."

"Of course," he replies and pulls out his business card, passing it to me. "You have a few days to decide what you'd like to do. You just give me a call if you need anything. I'm very sorry for your loss."

With that, they both tip their hats to me and leave, and I just stand here, staring at nothing.

"Did that just happen?"

"I'm afraid so," Drake says from beside me. "I'm sorry, Hannah Banana."

"I'm not sorry." I turn to face him, fierce anger burning through me. "It's just a blessing that he didn't kill anyone else this time. What the fuck was he doing in Montana anyway?"

"I don't know," Drake says. "Hannah—"

"No." I shake my head and stomp away. "I'm so damn pissed. How *dare* he come to my home? *My home.* What did he think he would do when he got here? That we'd have a great reunion, and break out some pictures and reminisce about the good ol' days? Because there weren't any good ol' days, Drake. None. And now they want me to claim his body?"

I laugh and pace around the living room.

"And do what with him? I don't give a rat's ass what happens to that body. And why shouldn't I abandon him?" I continue, seeing red and feeling palpitations begin in my chest. "He abandoned me my *whole life.* And then he killed my mother."

My breathing is harsh, and I can feel tears wetting my cheeks.

"Hannah, you need to sit down," Grace says, but I shake my head. I'm too wound up.

"I don't understand why he couldn't just stay in Kansas, in his pathetic life. I am fine without him. I'm better than fine. I'm fucking fantastic."

I stop to breathe, and realize that I'm having chest pains.

Fuck.

"I've worked myself up into a heart attack."

"What?" Grace demands and rushes to my side. "What's happening?"

"Chest pain. Short of breath." I look to Drake, but he's just watching me intently, not saying anything. "You're never this stoic."

"I'm letting you be angry."

"I'm not angry, I'm fucking furious. I don't need this." I let my head fall back. "I can't die. I just found the love of my life. This isn't fair."

"You're not dying," Drake says. "You're having an anxiety attack."

"Fuck that," I retort and glare at him. "I'm having *chest pain and shortness of breath.* You went to med school."

"I did, and I also know those are symptoms of an anxiety attack."

"That's not what this is," I insist and sit on a chair, holding my chest.

"Maybe I should call 911," Grace says, but I immediately shake my head.

"No, if you do that, they'll tell Brad. I don't want him to see me like this."

"Hannah, he's the love of your life as you just put it," Grace says. "If I didn't call Jacob at a time like this, he'd spank my ass red, and not in a fun way."

"Kinky," Drake murmurs, trying to make me laugh, but it's not working. "Hannah, take a deep breath."

"I can't." I push my head between my knees and bury my face in my hands, completely mortified. This is how I'm going out. Of a heart attack in my early thirties because my father decided to kill himself on a highway in Montana.

Someone presses a cold rag to the back of my neck, momentarily making me feel better, but then the pain shoots down my left arm and I'm officially freaked the fuck out.

"I have left arm pain." I stare up at Drake, truly scared now. "Drake, this isn't normal."

He sighs and nods. "Okay. I still don't think it's a heart attack, but we should take you in to be checked out, just to be sure."

I nod and stand, letting the business card I've been clutching in my hand fall to the floor. I don't bother with my handbag or phone, or even my keys as I follow Drake out of my house to his car.

"I'm going to call Brad," Grace says, but I turn on her and point my finger in her face.

"No." I shake my head. "*No*, Grace. Do not do that."

CHAPTER EIGHTEEN

Brad

"WOW, YOU'VE DONE A lot since I was here last." I'm standing with Jenna at the tree house project, our hands on our hips, staring up at the structures that finally look like a tree house. The siding is cedar shingles, and they look like they've been here all along. Like they belong on this mountain.

"It's amazing what you can get done when you fire a deadbeat and have someone on staff who knows what they're doing." She smiles sweetly, and motions for me to follow her into the biggest of the three buildings.

I'm stunned to see kitchen cabinets already installed and workers bustling about, measuring for the countertops that will be delivered in the morning.

"Blue cabinets?"

"I know, aren't they great?" she says with a big smile. "The countertops will be white, and it's really going to pop."

"If you say so."

"I do." She picks up a clipboard and starts reading through her checklist. "So you and Hannah had fun at Max's place?"

"We did. Have you ever been down there?"

"No, I keep meaning to, but something always comes up with one of the rentals." She shrugs. "I'll get there eventually."

"You should hire a management company to help you." This is an argument that's been happening for about two years now, ever since Jenna decided to branch out from the B&B and add other vacation rentals to her list of properties. "How many properties do you have now?"

"Twelve, if you include these," she says. "And yes, it's a full time job, but I love it. I have a manager at the B&B now, so that pretty much runs itself. I trust Maggie completely with it. So, I oversee the building of the homes, the design, and the rentals. I have housekeepers."

"I should hope so," I reply and shake my head at her. "You know, just hiring a management company to oversee the housekeeping and scheduling the rentals would be a huge help."

"I know." She sighs and rubs her forehead. "I know I'm being stubborn. But I *love* this stuff. Real estate is my jam, and greeting guests when they check in is a kick. They're excited to be there. And the personal touches I put on everything is what keeps them all coming back."

"There's no doubt that you're great at your job, Jen. You absolutely are."

"I'm going to see how it goes with these," she says, gesturing to the tree houses. "If they're as high maintenance as I think they will be, I'll have to hire someone to at least oversee the properties in Whisper."

Whisper is a neighboring town, only ten miles away, that is much bigger than Cunningham Falls and houses all of the amenities that our little town just can't, such as chain restaurants and department stores.

"How many are over there?"

"Six," she says. "So, I might need help down there. We'll see. For now, I'm content."

"That's the important thing."

"And now that you've distracted me from talking about your trip, spill it. Don't tell me about the sex."

"There's not much of anything else to tell." I grin when she wrinkles her nose and makes a gagging sound. "I mean, there was a *lot* of sex."

"Ew, really?"

"Well, there was, but there was other stuff too. We walked the beach a few times, watched whales. There's a great pool area, and the restaurants are great. We didn't leave the resort the whole time we were there."

"That sounds like the best vacation."

I nod and raise an eyebrow. "Maybe it's time for you to take a vacation."

"I don't have anyone to take a romantic vacation with," she reminds me.

"It's not like you put yourself out there, Jenna. You work and you go home."

"I'm not discussing my dating life with you."

"Fine." I sigh and then smile when she passes me a paper bag. "What's this?"

"I went to *Little Deli* earlier for sandwiches for the guys, and I got too many. You might as well take them for the guys."

"I'll take them over to Hannah's. She has Grace and Drake there to help her pack up the rest of her things."

"Why?"

"I told you that she moved in with me."

"No." She frowns. "You told me she was *going* to move in with you, and I assumed that meant in the coming months, not ten minutes later."

"Is this a problem?"

She blinks, thinking it over. "No. It's not a problem. You know I love Hannah, and I think she's good for you. I'm just surprised at the speed that you made it happen. You're usually more... laid back."

"I want her with me." I turn to leave. "Thanks for the sandwiches. I'll take them over to her now."

I saw her four hours ago, and I feel like I'm going through withdrawals. My friends would say I'm whipped.

And they wouldn't be wrong.

I enjoy her more than I ever thought I could. Spending time with her is the highlight of my day, and when we're apart, I count down until I get to see her again.

She's the best part of my life, and I'm relieved that she agreed to move in with me. Spending every night with her has been amazing.

She's at her old place today with Grace and Drake, finishing up with some packing and clearing out so we can get it ready for vacation rentals. I park at the curb in front of her house, pleased to see her car in the driveway. I reach for the brown bag full of lunch and climb out of the truck. It's quiet as I approach the house. The front door is open, with just the screen door shut, but maybe they're busy packing and aren't talking.

That would be unusual for Hannah and Grace, but not impossible.

"Hello?" I step inside and frown. Boxes are half packed, packing tape is sitting about, but no one is here. I call out again and walk to the back of the house, through the kitchen to the backyard, but still no one.

"What the hell?"

I dial Hannah's number and feel my heart start to beat faster when I hear it ring in the living room.

She doesn't have her phone. The house is open, her car is in the driveway.

What the fuck is going on?

I stalk into the living room to get her phone. No calls or texts that would give me a clue as to where she is.

I glance down and see a business card on the floor.

"Montana Highway Patrol, Vern Peterson."

For the first time in my life, my palms are starting to sweat as I dial Peterson's number and wait for him to answer.

"This is Brad Hull, the police chief of Cunningham Falls, and I'm looking for Hannah Malone. I found your business card in her home."

"I spoke with her today," he confirms.

"About what?"

"I can't tell you that, but I can tell you that when I saw her an hour ago she was fine."

I scowl. "She was here an hour ago? Do you know where she went?"

"No, Chief. Sorry. She was there when we left."

I thank him and hang up, more frustrated than before. What the hell is happening? And why did the highway patrol need to speak with her?

I try calling Grace's number and curse a blue streak when she doesn't answer.

I don't like not knowing where she is. Not like

this. Something is very wrong.

I'm pacing the living room when a number I don't recognize calls my phone.

"Hull."

"This is Drake. I think you should know that I'm with Hannah at the emergency room."

"Is she hurt?"

I'm already running out to my truck and driving toward the hospital, which is thankfully just ten minutes away.

"No," he says. "Let me know when you get here."

He hangs up and I toss my phone on the seat, run my hand over my face, and pray for patience. I run into the emergency room, stopping at the nurse's station.

"Fran, I need to get back to see Hannah."

Fran, a woman I've known most of my life, just frowns. "I'm not at liberty to give you any information on who may or may not be here."

"Don't fuck with me, I know she's here. Drake called me. I need to get back to her."

"I can't do that," she repeats. "It's family only, and you're not her husband."

"Neither is Drake."

"He escorted her here."

"I'm the chief of police."

Fran smiles, but I can see that I'm getting nowhere. "That doesn't matter here. This isn't a police matter, and I'm not letting you back there."

"I'll push my way through."

"I'd love to see you try. I've stopped men far bigger than you, Brad Hull." She props her hands on her hips, her chin the air, standing firm.

"Damn it, Fran."

"Go find a seat, and I'll come find you when and if you can go back."

I turn away just as Drake comes out to the waiting room.

"Thank God," I say when he approaches. "Nurse Ratchet here wouldn't let me back."

"I heard that," Fran says, but I ignore her.

"Hannah is safe and unharmed," Drake begins and pushes his hand through his hair.

"You're not making me feel any better."

"She doesn't know I called you, and frankly, she'll punch me in the balls when she finds out I did."

"Why?"

He shrugs. "I suspect she's embarrassed, but you should be here. The highway patrolmen showed up at the house to inform her that her father died."

"Shit."

"He was in Montana."

My eyes meet Drake's grim ones. "In Montana."

He nods. "I think she should tell you the rest because it's not my story to tell, but she's pretty upset. Not that her dad died, but it triggered some anxiety, and—"

"I get it."

"She doesn't look great, so I want you to prepare yourself for that. I haven't seen her this bad before."

I nod. "Understood. Now take me back there."

Drake leads me through the doors, despite a glaring Fran. I walk into a room to find Grace sitting next to Hannah, who has deep purple circles around her eyes, her red hair a riot around her, and her face blotchy from crying.

"Hey, sweetheart."

Rather than get angry, or order me out, she just breaks down in tears. She covers her face and cries, and I simply sit next to her and pull her into my arms, holding her close.

I should be hurt that she didn't want me here. I should be angry.

But all I feel is love, and relief that she's okay.

"Someone is about to come get her for a chest x-ray," Drake says as Grace stands. "We'll be in the waiting room if you need us."

I nod and hold Hannah against my chest, letting her cry it out.

The door closes, and she says, "I'm dying."

274 | KRISTEN PROBY

I frown and pull her away from me so I can look into her blue eyes. "Excuse me?"

"Heart attack," she says, and my world falls away.

"You're having a damn heart attack?" I press the call button for the nurse and stare blindly at the monitors. "Drake said you're okay."

A woman bustles into the room. "How can we help?"

"If she's having a heart attack, shouldn't someone be in here?"

"We don't think that's what's happening," she says with a smile. "We have labs drawn, heart monitor going, and she's about to get a chest x-ray. Right now, in fact."

A young man comes in and ushers me off the bed so he can wheel her out to a nearby lab. He doesn't ask her to get up, but instead does all of the work with her lying on the bed. After the x-ray is taken, he asks if we'd like to see the images.

"Yes," Hannah says immediately and stands so she can see his monitor.

"This looks pretty standard, although I'm no radiologist."

"No, look." She points at a spot where her lungs are. "This is a tumor."

"I think those are blood vessels," the tech says. "I've done hundreds of these, and those are blood vessels."

Hannah just shakes her head and gets back on the bed, looking defeated. "Please take me back to my room."

She's wheeled back, and hooked back up to her monitors. After a few moments, the doctor comes in and sits at Hannah's bedside.

"I have good news, Dr. Malone. Your labs have all come back normal so far. I'm waiting on one more enzyme lab, but I expect that to be normal as well. Your EKG and chest x-ray are both in normal limits."

"I don't know how that can be," Hannah says with true confusion on her face. "I saw the tumor on the x-ray. Didn't you see it?"

The doctor frowns and opens her laptop, bringing up the x-ray in question and turns the computer so Hannah can see it. "Where?"

"Here." She points to the cluster in the center of her lung.

"Those are blood vessels."

"Bullshit," Hannah mutters and shakes her head. "It's cancer. I'm having a goddamn heart attack and I have cancer and you're doing *nothing*. I want a second opinion."

"Hannah, I promise you, you're not dying."

Tears are streaming down her sweet face, and it makes me ache. She's devastated. She's convinced.

And it doesn't matter that she's a doctor. All of her training and common sense are gone, replaced by the reactions of a scared woman.

I don't know what to do for her, but I know I'm not going anywhere.

Not now, not ever.

She looks up at me with tears rolling out of her blue eyes and says, "I don't know what to do. What do I do?"

CHAPTER NINETEEN

Hannah

"**H**ANNAH, LISTEN TO ME," Dr. Linderman says, catching my attention. "This is *not* a tumor. And I'm watching the monitor right now. Your heart is steady and just fine. I'm not lying to you."

"It's fluttering right now," I reply, so fucking frustrated that no one believes me. And even more frustrated that I can't stop the nonsense running through my head.

I can't remember any of my medical training. None of it.

"Flutters happen with anxiety," she replies, and I just stare at her in horror. I've spent the past two hours here for *nothing*. All because of this stupid anxiety.

"I'm so sorry," I whisper. She pats my hand and smiles kindly.

"You don't have anything to be sorry for."

"My left hand feels weird."

"You're tense. I'm quite sure the nerves to your

arm are being pinched, and that's causing the dis-
comfort."

"So, I'm *not* having a heart attack."

"No. You're not. I'm going to wait for that last
lab, and then you're free to go."

She smiles and leaves the room, and I can't
look Brad in the face.

I'm humiliated.

"Baby," he says. "Look at me."

"I'm so embarrassed."

"You don't need to be." He sits on the bed with
me again and pulls me into his arms, which makes
me feel better. "It sounds like all of the symptoms
felt like a heart attack. I would have been scared
myself."

I nod, but then take a deep breath and swallow
hard.

"Here's the thing, Brad. I can't turn this off. I
can't make it stop. I'm a trained professional, but
when this starts, all of my training goes out the
window and rational thought goes with it. I'm *sure*
that something is wrong. Everyone thinks it's funny. Or cute."

I wipe a tear off my cheek.

"Drake will make a joke, or brush it off, and I'll
play along. But it's not funny." I lift my eyes to his
now and have to bite my lip so I can pull myself
together, even a little bit. "It's not funny. It's scary.
I will go a long time without anything like this hap-

pening, but it's always, *always* in the back of my mind that something is wrong. Headache? I must have a brain tumor. Lower abdominal pain? Ovarian cancer. I'm a hot mess, Brad, and I wouldn't blame you in the least if you bailed now. I would."

"No, you wouldn't," he says quietly.

Okay, I wouldn't. But I wouldn't blame him if he did.

He kisses my temple and then reaches to grab a stethoscope off the countertop.

"Here, put these in your ears."

I do as I'm told and wipe my nose on a tissue. Brad holds the other end over his own chest and I immediately hear his heart, strong and sure in my ears.

"Do you hear that?"

"Of course."

"Close your eyes." I do as I'm told, and he begins to talk. I'm swept up in the sound of his deep voice, his strong arms wrapped around me and his heart beating in my ears. "This is the heart of a man who loves you more than he ever thought he could. I didn't know what I was missing until you came into my life, Hannah. This heart believes in you, admires you, and takes so much joy in you."

Tears continue to fall down my face, but I don't care. I press my cheek to Brad's shoulder and keep listening.

"When I thought my heart would break earlier

this summer, when I had to tell a friend that his child was gone, you were there to help me recover from that. You held me, and you soothed the pain, Han. This is a grateful heart."

He pauses and kisses my temple.

"This heart is strong. Listen to how steady it beats, how sure it is. It's brave and true, and it always does the right thing, even when it's hard. It's healthy, Hannah. So healthy. It's going to beat for many more years to come."

I open my eyes and am surprised to discover that at some point he moved the stethoscope to my own chest. The strong, healthy heart I've been listening to is my own.

"You always manage to make me feel better. You bring so much to my life, Brad."

"Do you still want me to bail?"

"No. I might trip you if you try to leave."

He kisses me again and sets the stethoscope aside. "You are not broken, sweetheart. You're not a hot mess. You're a human being, and sometimes life is just hard."

"Yeah. I feel bad for Drake and Grace. They were there when the patrolmen came."

"I'm glad they were," he admits. "I'd hate to think what would have happened if you'd been alone."

"My dad died."

He nods, and I assume that Drake told him.

"He's been dead to me for a long time. I'm not terribly sad that he's gone. Does that make me a bad person?"

His lips twitch into a smile. "No. You're not a bad person."

"They said that I'm the only surviving relative, so I'm responsible for his body." I swallow hard. "I don't want to deal with that."

"You don't have to. There are options." He cups my face in his hand gently. "Is it that he was in Montana that triggered all of this?"

"Probably," I admit, feeling angry about that again, but not willing to throw myself into another episode. "He was coming here to try to get something from me. It wasn't any other reason. He was probably broke. But I would have told him no and sent him packing.

"I hate that he was so close to my home. I made a place for myself here, far away from him and all of the chaos he caused. I made a way for myself in this world without him. He wasn't welcome to invade the safety of the life I've built."

"That makes sense," Brad says. "We'll deal with it, together. Just like we dealt with this together."

"I didn't want you here," I admit, and he cocks a brow. "Grace said if she pulled something like that, Jacob would spank her ass red."

"I'm considering it," he replies, and my eyes whip up to his. "You scared me. And when I arrived, they wouldn't let me back to see you because I'm not family."

"I didn't think of that. Grace wanted to call you, but I wouldn't let her. It goes back to what I said earlier, I didn't want you to have to see me like this. It's embarrassing."

"If I were in an accident, and cut my leg open, would it make sense to you that I wouldn't want you in the emergency room with me because I was embarrassed about the way it happened?"

"How did it happen?" I ask, playing devil's advocate.

"You're missing the point."

"No," I confess. "It wouldn't make sense and I'd be tearing the place apart to get to you."

"I was about to try that, but Fran says she can take me and I'm inclined to believe her."

I laugh at the thought of the little nurse going up against Brad.

"I'm glad you came."

"Sadie hasn't left my side since we got home."

It's several hours later, and I'm curled up on the couch with Sadie's head in my lap. She's snoozing and I just can't stop crying. She wakes up now and again to check on me, whimpers a bit, and then falls back to sleep.

"She loves you," Brad says just as the doorbell

rings.

"That hasn't been good luck today." I lay my head back on the couch, fighting off the crying-induced headache.

"It's pizza," Brad says as he comes in the room. "From Drake. There's a note on the box that says he hopes you're feeling better."

"That was sweet." My stomach growls, and I realize I'm hungry. "I guess it's good timing."

"Do you enjoy pineapple on your pizza?" Brad asks after opening the box.

"Oh yeah."

"Maybe we have to rethink this whole living together situation."

"You mean, you *don't* love pineapple on piz-za?"

"It's too sweet," he says, but then smiles. "But it's just on half. Drake's not stupid."

I grin and watch him walk into the open kitchen to get us plates, and wouldn't you know it, the tears start again.

I can't fucking turn them off.

My eyes are ridiculous. They're puffy and purple, and I look like I went a round with a heavy-weight champ. I keep rubbing them because I can't turn the tears off.

It's a vicious circle.

"I don't even know what I'm crying about anymore."

"It's your body cleansing itself," Brad assures me and passes me a plate. The aroma wakes Sadie out of a dead sleep, and she's immediately ordered onto the floor.

"Are you the doctor now?" I ask.

"No, just guessing." He takes a bite and watches me. "I don't like seeing you like this."

"I know, it's pretty bad."

"No, I just don't like to see you cry."

We're about halfway into our pizza when the doorbell rings again.

"This time it's flowers," Brad says, carrying them into the living room and setting them on the table next to me. I pull the card out and open it.

"Hannah,

By the time you read this, we hope you're feeling much better!

Love,

Grace and Jacob"

"That was nice." I wipe the tear from under my eye, and then the doorbell rings *again*. "I can't take much more of this."

He laughs and goes to answer it. He's gone longer this time, but then returns with a bag from my favorite ice cream shop and a card.

"Huckleberry?" I ask.

"Of course."

I read this card.

Hannah,

Just a reminder that I love you!

Jenna

"Is everyone trying to make me cry today?"

"I don't think that's hard to do, sweetheart." He sets the ice cream in the freezer and returns to his pizza. "I think your friends are just worried about you."

"It's amazing. I've always known that I belong here. I don't know how to describe it, other than I knew I was home when I got here. But over the past few months, I've finally begun to feel like I'm a part of the community. I have an amazing network of friends, and your family makes me feel welcome."

"They all care about you."

I nod and take another bite of pizza, then set it aside and crawl into his lap. "I think that at first they cared about me because they love *you.* But now they love me too, and it's a really good feeling."

His arms tighten around me. The fear and anger from earlier are gone now, and I'm left with so much gratitude.

Love.

I straddle him and settle against him, feeling him harden.

"I love you," I whisper.

"I love you back," he whispers in return, making me grin. I wiggle out of my sweatpants, unfasten his jeans and set him free, then lower myself onto him, making us both sigh in pure delight.

"You make me feel things, Brad. Big things."

"It is impressive, isn't it?"

I blink at him, then let out a big laugh. I wrap my arms around his neck and ride him, enjoying him. Soaking him in.

"Yes, perv, it's impressive."

CHAPTER TWENTY

Hannah

Two Months Later

"HOW WAS YOUR DAY, DEAR?" Brad asks as I walk in the house from work. He beat me home today, and if my nose isn't deceiving me, he's made spaghetti for dinner.

Good God, I love this man.

"It was pretty good. I had two hysterectomies today, and I thought I was going to have to stay a bit late for a delivery, but it came about an hour ago."

"That baby knew that you had a sexy guy to go home to."

"Yes. That must be it. And then I saw my therapist for an hour, and I'm glad I'm going. He's helping a lot." I giggle and turn my face up for a kiss. He takes it from an innocent peck to a hot, searing make out sesh in about one-point-six seconds. "Mm, I missed you, too."

He winks at me and returns to his work station, chopping up vegetables for a salad.

"I grabbed the mail on my way in," I announce and sort through it, setting his mail to the side. There's an envelope from the school of medicine that I graduated from, and I immediately open it. "Wow."

"What is it?"

"A thank you letter," I reply and read it out loud.

Dr. Malone,

It is with great respect and appreciation that I write this letter to thank you for your donation to the Yale School of Medicine. For generations, taking anatomy classes has been a rite of passage for medical students, and this integral part of becoming a physician would be lost without the opportunity that donors such as yourself have given us.

We take great pride in knowing that you believe that we can make great changes in the future of medicine. The donation of your family member is something we hold near and dear to our hearts and use the greatest care as we use them to teach future generations of physicians.

On a personal note, you were one of my students in your second year here at Yale, and I wanted to offer my sincerest condolences and personal gratitude.

Sincerely,

Matthew T. Murdoch, M.D., Ph.D.

I fold the letter and return it to its envelope as Brad walks around the island to wrap an arm around my back.

"Are you okay with this?"

"Yes. Absolutely." I nod and smile up at him. "I know that I did the right thing in not abandoning him and instead donating his remains to science. I finally have a reason to be proud of my dad, and he's *finally* a productive member of society."

Brad smiles and returns to his vegetables.

"I think your dad would be happy with that."

"I don't know if he would, but my mom would be, and that's something too. Now, I'm starving, and that smells fantastic."

"It's a family recipe."

"Spaghetti?"

"That's right."

I glance at the empty jar of store bought spaghetti sauce and snort. "Are you a descendent of Ragu?"

"No, smart ass. You use that as the base, and then add other things to make it more delicious."

"If you say so. Gimme."

"You're very demanding." But he smiles and dishes up a helping of the steaming sauce and pasta. It does smell fantastic. "Here you go."

I take a bite and chew slowly as he watches, knowing that he wants me to offer him a reaction.

I swallow and shrug a shoulder. "It's pretty good."

"Just pretty good?"

"Okay," I say with a smile. "It's *really* good. I hope there will be enough for leftovers."

"I made a ton," he says and dishes up his own plate.

"I have a favor to ask."

"Anything."

"After dinner, do you mind taking me down to the lake? It's a nice day and it's not anywhere near dark yet."

"Of course." He takes a bite of his own dinner. "We can go anywhere you like."

"Just the lake."

We're both hungry, so dinner disappears quickly. We stack our dirty dishes in the sink for later and head out in his truck for the public access beach.

"It's so nice since most of the tourists have gone home," I remark, enjoying the way the sunlight bounces off the water.

"Even OPTS is over."

"OPTS?"

"Old people tourist season. Haven't you noticed that about the time that school starts and the families go home, that's when the old people come in for the last half of September?"

"No," I reply with a giggle. "Is this really a

thing?"

"Hell yes, it's a thing. I can't even begin to tell you how many elderly people we pull over in the early fall. It's ridiculous."

"I've never heard of such a thing," I reply as he pulls to a stop by the boat launch dock at Whitetail Lake. "Let's go sit on the dock."

He gives me a weird look, then says, "Okay."

He follows me down the long dock over the water to the very end. I sit down, careful to not put my feet near the water, and he joins me.

"It's a beautiful evening," I say again, grappling for conversation.

"Yes. Did you bring me here to break up with me?"

My gaze whips up to his, but he's smiling down at me.

"No. Not even close."

"Good. What's up, Hannah?"

I swallow hard and look down at the water. "I think I need to put my feet in this water."

He's quiet beside me for a moment, and then he reaches over and takes my hand in his, linking our fingers.

"Why?" he asks softly.

"Because I'm afraid of it, and I don't need to be." I lift my chin and look at him. "Because you've helped me conquer so many fears this year, and this is one that I need to be gone so I can enjoy our lake again. I want to be able to kayak and boat and swim in it next year with our friends without being afraid.

"I'm so fucking tired of being afraid."

"Okay." He nods and looks down at the water, then back at me. "How do you want to do this?"

"I don't have any idea." I blow out a breath with a humorless laugh. "When I'm hiking in the woods, afraid that I'll get attacked by a grizzly bear, I just march fast ahead, intent on getting through it alive."

"Well, you could just take the plunge, literally, and put your feet in there."

"I don't think it's that simple." I chew my bottom lip for a moment, thinking it over. "Tell me again about how they decided that it's safe."

"Well, first they turned off all of the power that runs under the lake, and then they used a grid to methodically comb the lake, diving down to see where the power lines were exposed."

"Why are there lines that run under the lake?"

"Because there are homes all around the lake, but not necessarily roads that access it all. The city is currently working on approving a road that would completely circle the lake, but we don't have that at this time. So, to make it more cost effective to feed power to all of the houses, they ran the lines through the lake, under the bottom of it where it's the most shallow, at the most narrow points."

"I see." I nod, looking out at the lake before us. The sun is just beginning to set, casting the mountains in pink. It's breathtaking. "And you believe that it's totally fixed, without any chance of it happening again?"

"I do believe that," he says, squeezing my hand. "Not only did they fix the problem, they spent weeks surveying every foot of the lines, making sure they're secure and safe. Hannah, I wouldn't let my townspeople near anything that could harm or kill them."

"I know that," I reply. "Remember, this isn't rational."

"It's okay." Most of the beach is deserted, except for a family walking their dog about two hundred yards away. The little girl has taken her shoes off and dips her feet in the water, giggling at how cold it is.

"A toddler can do it," I murmur and then look back out at the water again. "Will you put your feet in with me?"

"So if we die, at least we die together?"

"Not funny." But then I laugh, unable to help myself. "Okay, it's funny. Yes. If one of us dies, we both die."

"I can do that." I slip out of my flip flops and he takes his shoes and socks off and looks at me. "Are you ready?"

"Hell no."

"We don't have to do this."

"Yes, we do." I purse my lips and dip my big toe in, then pull back fast. "Not even a zap."

"All right, the whole foot now. Let's do this."

I nod, and we both sink one foot into the water. It's cold and feels good on my skin, between my toes.

And I didn't die.

I sigh, feeling like a huge weight has been lifted off of my shoulders. I sink the other foot in with it and let them dangle, swishing around.

"I'm still here."

"Thank goodness," he says, still holding my hand. I don't feel foolish, I feel powerful. "I'm *so* proud of you."

I look up to find his green eyes happy, full of pride, and sexy as hell, just as they always are.

"You know what? Me too. Let's go home."

The End

About Kristen Proby

Kristen was born and raised in a small resort town in her beloved Montana. In her mid-twenties, she decided to stretch her wings and move to the Pacific Northwest, where she made her home for more than a dozen years.

During that time, Kristen wrote many romance novels and joined organizations such as RWA and other small writing groups. She spent countless hours in workshops, and more mornings than she can count up before the dawn so she could write before going to work. She submitted many manuscripts to agents and editors alike, but was always told no. In the summer of 2012, the self-publishing scene was new and thriving, and Kristen had one goal: to publish just one book. It was something she longed to cross off of her bucket list.

Not only did she publish one book, she's since published close to thirty titles, many of which have hit the USA Today, New York Times and Wall Street Journal Bestsellers lists. She continues to self publish, best known for her With Me In Seattle and Boudreaux series, and is also proud to work with William Morrow, a division of HarperCollins, with the Fusion Series.

Kristen and her husband, John, make their home in her hometown of Whitefish, Montana with their two pugs and two cats.

Website
www.kristenproby.com
Facebook
www.facebook.com/BooksByKristenProby
Twitter
twitter.com/Handbagjunkie
Goodreads
goodreads.com/author/show/6550037.Kristen_Proby

Other Books by Kristen Proby

The Big Sky Series
Charming Hannah
Kissing Jenna
Waiting for Willa – Coming soon

The Fusion Series
Listen To Me
Close To You
Blush For Me
The Beauty of Us
Savor You

The Boudreaux Series
Easy Love
Easy Charm
Easy Melody
Easy Kisses
Easy Magic
Easy Fortune
Easy Nights

The With Me In Seattle Series
Come Away With Me
Under the Mistletoe With Me
Fight With Me
Play With Me
Rock With Me
Safe With Me
Tied With Me

Breathe With Me
Forever With Me
The Love Under the Big Sky Series
Loving Cara
Seducing Lauren
Falling For Jillian
Saving Grace

From 1001 Dark Nights
Easy With You
Easy For Keeps
No Reservations
Tempting Brooke

The Romancing Manhattan Series
All the Way

If you're new to the Big Sky gang, here's a look
at the very beginning with Loving Cara!

LOVING
CARA

PROLOGUE
Spring

Josh

THE CELL PHONE ON my belt vibrates against my hip, and I pull it from its holster, register my dad's name on the caller ID, and answer.

"What's up, Dad?"

"Where are you, Josh?" His voice is hard but calm, and all the hairs on my body immediately stand on end.

"I'm checking fence on the far-west pasture, about fifteen minutes from the house."

"We need you here, Son."

"Is Mom okay?" My voice is calm, and just as hard as Dad's. We're nothing if not calm in a crisis.

"She's fine, but we have a situation."

"I'm on my way."

Holstering the phone, I kick Magic gently and she immediately sets off in a gallop toward the house.

What the fuck is going on?

The last time Dad called with that tone in his voice, my brother, Zack, had been hurt in Afghanistan.

He's in Afghanistan now.

Before long, the old, sprawling house comes into view. Although mostly retired, Mom and Dad still live in the big house, and I rebuilt one of the old farmhand houses on the opposite side of the property a few years ago. I'm in charge of the Lazy K Ranch now, and I love every minute of it.

Mom and Dad step out onto the porch as I dismount, and suddenly I hear tires on the gravel driveway.

"What's going on?" I demand, scowling as I watch my dad's eyes go hard. A blue rental pulls to a stop in front of us.

"Kensie called," he mutters.

"How could she do this to him?" Mom whispers with tears in her eyes. "To both of them?"

"Would someone like to tell me what in the hell is going on?"

"Get out of the car, Seth."

I know that voice. Ice instantly runs through my veins as I turn to see Zack's wife, Kensie, pull herself out of the passenger seat, open the back door, and pull my nephew, Seth, out of the car, along with a duffel bag, which she throws without care onto the dirt.

"What's this about?"

"Seth's your problem now," she replies coldly.

My eyes immediately fall on the boy, who's looking down and drawing circles in the gravel with the toe of his worn shoe. His jeans are a size too small, the hem riding above his ankles, and his T-shirt is stained and dirty.

"Seth isn't a problem," Mom replies, and flies down the stairs to pull Seth into her arms. He stiffens, but doesn't pull away. He also doesn't hug her back.

Jesus, he was here two years ago, bright-eyed and interested in all of the ranch animals. Now his eyes are dull and tired.

"He is for me," Kensie replies with a shrug. Her clothes are impeccable, and I assume purposefully a size too small. Her hair and nails are polished and perfect. She winks over at me and my stomach rolls in revulsion. "How are you, handsome?"

"What is this about?"

"Zack made noise about wanting a divorce the last time he called from BFE, so I beat him to the punch. Cole"—she gestures toward the car and the man sitting impatiently inside—"doesn't want a kid around, and frankly, I'm tired of being a full-time mom."

"You're tired of being a full-time mom?" I yell. Dad shakes his head and my mom tries to pull Seth away and into the house, but Dad puts his hand on her shoulder, stopping her.

Seth shouldn't have to hear this bullshit.

"Twelve years I have been alone with him," she sneers, and points her finger at her son. "While Zack spent more time in a desert or in a plane with the army, leaving us in a different city every two years. I stayed because Zack's paychecks were nice, and I didn't have to work, but I'm done. I sold his car." Dad gasps and I want to wrap my hands around her little neck and squeeze. Zack loves that damn car. "I gave the rest of his shit to charity and I'm giving you the kid. If Zack wants to traipse around the world every year and ignore his family, fine, but I'm done! I deserve more than this!"

She's screaming now, carrying on about what is owed to her, but I can't take my eyes off Seth. His face hasn't shown one bit of emotion. Most kids would be in tears, horrified by their mother's behavior.

How long has this been going on?

"Seth is always welcome here," I begin, and take a few steps toward Kensie, satisfied when she shuts her foul mouth and her eyes go round as I get closer.

I've never enjoyed scaring women. It's easy for me to do with my size and is something I've always been careful of.

But I'm going to scare the shit out of her.

"But you are not. Seth will stay with us until Zack is back in the States in a few months. You are never to come back here." I step closer and loom over her. "If you ever show your face here again, I'll have you arrested for trespassing and I will ruin your pathetic life."

Her eyes widen and her jaw drops in surprise as she takes half a step away from me, but she quickly pulls herself together and squares her shoulders, pulling her painted-on eyebrows into a scowl.

"Why would I ever come back here? There's nothing here I want." She raises her chin defiantly and, without a look at Seth, climbs in the car, which peels out of the driveway.

"Oh, honey," Mom whispers, and kisses Seth's hair. He shrugs and pulls away, grabs his bag, and looks up at me for the first time since they drove up.

"Can I stay here, Uncle Josh?" His eyes flick over to Magic and back to me. He always loved the horses.

"Of course, buddy, you always have a place here."

He nods soberly and looks back down at the ground, waiting to be told what to do. Mom is openly crying now, and Dad just shakes his head, wipes his hand down his face, and sighs. "Come on, Seth. Grandpa will show you to your room. You can have your dad's old room."

"I don't want anything of his," Seth spits out, his hands in fists. "I'd rather sleep in the barn."

Dad blinks in surprise, glances to both Mom

and me, then frowns. "Okay, the spare room it is then."

"Come on, honey, let's get you settled and I'll fix you some lunch." Mom smiles at Seth through her tears and wraps an arm around his thin shoulders. "We've missed you so much. There are some fish out in the creek that need to be caught, you know...." Her voice fades away as the three of them walk into the house, and all I can do is stand here, my hands on my hips, and wonder what the fuck just happened, and what are we going to do with a twelve-year-old boy?

CHAPTER ONE
Early summer

Cara

"CARA, DO YOU HAVE a minute?" My boss, Kyle Reardon, pokes his head in my open classroom door and offers me a warm smile.

"Sure, what's up?"

He saunters in and takes a long look around my empty classroom. The breeze from the open windows ruffles his hair, and he runs his hand through it as he leans against my desk. "Looks like you're ready to get out of here for a few months." He gazes down at me warmly. "Remember last week when you mentioned that you'd be up for a tutoring job this summer?" I roll back in my chair and look up at him. He's handsome, with short copper hair and blue eyes, a nice build.

He's also married with four children.

"I do," I confirm.

"Well, I have one for you."

"Who?"

"You know the King family, right? They run that big ranch just outside of town."

"Of course, I grew up here, Kyle," I reply dryly. In a town the size of Cunningham Falls, Montana, we pretty much all know each other, especially those of us who grew up here, just as our parents did, and their parents before them.

"Zack's boy, Seth, needs a tutor this summer."

"Zack's back in town?" I ask, my eyebrows raised in surprise.

"I don't think so." Kyle shakes his head and shrugs. "I can't tell you their business, small town or not. Seth is staying with Jeff and Nancy, and Josh is helping too."

"Oh," I mutter, surprised. "So for whom would I be working, exactly?"

"So proper," Kyle teases me, and grins. "You'll be working for Josh. You can go straight to his place on Monday morning. They'd like you to come Monday through Friday, about nine till noon."

"Geez, he must need a lot of tutoring."

The laughter leaves Kyle's eyes and he sighs. "He's a really smart kid, but he's stubborn and has a bit of an attitude. I'm warning you, he's not an easy kid to work with. He's only been here for three months. He refuses to do the work or hand it in."

"Does he start trouble?" I steeple my fingers in front of me, thinking.

"No, he just keeps to himself. Doesn't say much to anyone."

I'll have to work with Josh King, which won't be difficult. He was always nice to me in high school, smiles at me in passing when I see him around town. He and his brother are nice guys.

Rumor has it he's a womanizer, but nice nonetheless.

And I'd be lying if I said I hadn't had a crush on him for as long as I can remember.

But I can be professional and teach Josh's nephew. I didn't really want to paint my entire house this summer, anyway.

"Okay, I'll give it a go."

"Great, thanks, Cara." Kyle stands and turns to leave my classroom. "Have a good summer!"

"You too!" I call after him as he goes whistling down the dark, deserted hallway.

Cool, I have a summer job.

I love my town. Like, wholeheartedly, never want to move away, love it. I don't understand how Jillian, my best friend since kindergarten, can stand living so far away in California. Our town is small, only about six thousand full-time residents, but the population doubles in the peak of summer and the heart of winter with tourists here for skiing, hiking, swimming, and all the other fun outdoor activities that the brochures brag about.

We sit in a valley surrounded by tall mountains, and when it's sunny, the sky is so big and blue it almost hurts the eyes.

I pull into the long gravel driveway off the highway just outside town and follow it past the large, white main house to the back of the property where Josh's house sits. It's not as big as the main house, but it's still large, bigger than my house in town, and is surrounded by tall evergreen trees and long lines of white wooden fences.

I do not envy the poor sap who has to paint the fences every few years.

The butterflies I've kept at bay come back with a vengeance, fluttering in my belly as I come to a stop in front of his house. Josh and his brother are twins, and until Zack broke his nose in football their senior year, it was almost impossible to tell them apart. They're both big guys, tall and broad-shouldered. Zack always had a more intense look in his face, while Josh is more laid-back, quick to smile or tease—especially me, it seemed. In high school I was invisible to most people, having been a little too round, a lot too plain, but Josh noticed me.

He used to pull on my horrible curls as he'd walk past me at school, and of course because he was two years ahead of me, and a football star, I was crazy about him. My hair naturally falls in tight ringlets, but I've since straightened it, thank God.

I haven't seen much of Josh over the years.

Each of us went away to college, and since we've both returned, I may catch a glimpse of him at the grocery store or in a restaurant, but never long enough to talk to him. I wonder if the rumors of his womanizing are true.

They were in high school.

I just hope he hasn't turned into one of those cowboys who wear tight Wrangler jeans and straw cowboy hats.

My lips twitch at the thought as I pull myself out of my compact Toyota. The front door swings open, and there he is, all six foot three of him. Only with great effort does my jaw not drop.

Jesus, we breed hot men in Montana.

Josh's hair is dark, dark brown and he has chocolate-colored eyes to match. His olive skin has acquired a deep tan, and when he smiles, he has a dimple in his left cheek that can melt panties at twenty paces.

Dark stubble is on his chin this morning, and he flashes that cocky smile as he steps onto the porch. His jeans—Levi's, not Wranglers—ride low on his hips, and a plain white T-shirt hugs his muscular chest and arms. I can't help but wonder what he smells like.

Down, girl.

Following directly behind Josh is a tall, blond woman I don't recognize, laughing at something he must have said just before he sauntered through the door. They stop on the covered front porch long enough for him to smile sweetly down at her. He pulls his large hand down her arm and says softly, "Have a good day, and good luck."

"Thanks, Josh," she responds, and bounces down the steps of the front porch, nods at me, and hops into her Jeep.

"Carolina Donovan," Josh murmurs, and stuffs his hands in his pockets.

"You know I hate it when you call me Carolina." I roll my eyes. "My parents should have been brought up on child-abuse charges for that name."

Josh laughs and shakes his head. "It's a beautiful name." He frowns and rocks back on his heels. "You look great, Cara."

"Uh, you've seen me around town over the years, Josh," I remind him with a half-smile. "I hope I didn't interrupt anything?" I grimace inside, regretting the question immediately. Mom always said, never ask a question you don't want the answer to.

He shrugs one shoulder and offers me that cocky grin. God, he's such a charmer. "Nah, we were finished."

I frown at him. What does that mean?

"So, where is Seth?" I ask, changing the subject.

Josh frowns in turn and looks toward the big house. "He should be on his way in a few minutes. I have to warn you, Cara, working with Seth may not be a day at the beach. He's a good kid, but he's having a rough time of it." Josh rubs his hand over his face and sighs.

"Why is he here and not with his mom?"

"Because the bitch dropped him off here so she can be footloose and fancy-free. She's filed for divorce. Good riddance. I wish she'd brought him to us years ago."

"Oh." I don't know what else to say. I never liked Kensie King. She was a bitch in high school, but she was pretty and popular, and I'm quite sure Zack never planned on knocking her up.

But none of that is Seth's fault.

"What areas does he need help in?" I ask, and pull my tote bag out of the passenger seat. When I turn around, Josh's eyes are on my ass and he's chewing on his lower lip. I frown and stand up straight, self-conscious of my round behind.

"Josh?"

"I'm sorry, what?" He shakes his head and narrows his eyes on my face.

"What areas does Seth need the most help in?"

"All of them. He failed every class this spring."

"Every class?" I ask incredulously.

"Yeah. He's a smart kid, I don't know what his problem is."

"I don't need a tutor!" a young male voice calls out. I turn to see Seth riding a BMX bike from the big house down the driveway.

"Seth, don't start." Josh's eyes narrow and he folds his arms over his chest. "Ms. Donovan is here to help. You will be nice."

Seth rolls his eyes and hops off the bike, laying it on its side, and mirrors his uncle's stance, arms crossed over his chest.

God, he looks just like his dad and his uncle. He could be their younger brother. He's going to inherit their height and has the same dark hair, but his eyes are hazel.

He's going to be a knockout someday.

And right now he's scowling at me.

"Hi, Seth. I'm Cara."

"What is it, Cara or Ms. Donovan?" he asks defiantly.

"Seth!" Josh begins, but I interrupt him. Seth isn't the first difficult child I've come across.

"Since it's summer, and I'm in your home, it's Cara. But if you see me at school, it's Ms. Donovan. Sound fair?"

Seth shrugs his slim shoulders and twists his lips as if he wants to say something smart but doesn't dare in his uncle's company.

Smart kid.

"Where do you want us?" I ask Josh, who is still glaring at Seth. They're clearly frustrated with each other.

"You can sit at the kitchen table. The house is empty during the day since I'm out working, so you shouldn't be interrupted." Josh motions for us to go in ahead of him, and as I walk past, he reaches out to pull my hair. "What happened to your curls?"

"I voted them off the island," I reply dryly, then almost trip as he laughs, sending shivers down my spine.

He leans in and whispers, "I liked them."

I shrug and follow Seth to the kitchen. "I didn't."

Josh's home is spacious; the floor plan is open from the living area right inside the front door through to the eat-in kitchen with its maple cabinets the color of honey and smooth, light granite countertops. The windows are wide and I can see all over the property from inside the main room.

I immediately feel at home here, despite the obvious bachelor-pad feel to it. Large, brown leather couches face a floor-to-ceiling river rock fireplace with a flat-screen TV mounted above it. Fishing, hunting, and men's-health magazines are scattered on the coffee table, along with an empty coffee mug. Not a throw pillow or knickknack to be found anywhere.

Typical guy.

Seth pulls a chair away from the table and plops down in it, resting his head on his folded arms.

"Seth, sit up." Josh is exasperated and Seth just sinks deeper into his slouch.

"I think we're good to go." I grin at Josh but he scowls.

"Are you sure?"

"Yep, we're good. You get to work and leave us be so we can, too."

I turn my back on him, dismissing him, and begin pulling worksheets, pens, and a book out of my bag.

"I'll be working nearby today, so just call my cell if you need me."

"Fine." I wave him off, not looking over at him. I sense him still standing behind me. Finally I turn and raise an eyebrow. "You're still here."

He's watching me carefully, leaning against the countertop, his rough hands tucked in his pockets. My eyes are drawn to his biceps, straining against the sleeves of his tee. "You got really pushy."

"I'm a teacher. It's either be pushy or die a long, slow death. Now go. We have work to do today."

"You'll have lunch with us before you go." Josh pushes himself away from the counter and saunters to the front door, grabs an old, faded-green baseball cap, and settles it backward on his head. "I'm pushy too."

He grins and that dimple winks at me before he leaves the house, shutting the door behind him.

Good God, I will not be able to focus if he doesn't leave us be while I'm here.

"You ready to get to work?" I ask Seth, thumbing through my writing worksheets until I find the one I want.

"This is a waste of time," he grumbles.

"Why do you say that?"

He shrugs again and buries his face in his arms.

"Well, I don't consider it a waste of time. What's your favorite subject?"

No answer.

"Least favorite?"

No answer.

"I personally like math, but I always sucked at it."

Seth shifts his head slightly and one eye peeks at me.

"Are you good at math?" I ask him.

"It's easy."

"Not for me." I sigh.

"But you're a teacher." Seth finally sits up and frowns at me.

"That doesn't mean I'm good at everything. Teachers aren't superhuman or anything."

"I can do math."

"Okay, let's start there."

Seth eyes me for a minute and then shrugs. It seems shrugging is his favorite form of communication.

"Are you really going to stay and have lunch?"

"Does that make you uncomfortable?" I pass him the math worksheet.

"No, I don't care." He picks up a pencil and starts marking the sheet, digging right in, and I grin.

"Does the food suck?"

"No, Gram packs us a lunch every day."

"Well then, I'll stay."

His lips twitch, but he doesn't smile—yet somehow I think I just won a big battle.

"So, looks like fried chicken and potato salad, homemade rolls, and fruit." Josh pulls the last of the food out of the ice chest and passes Seth a Coke.

"Your mom goes all out."

"She's been making lunch for ranch hands for almost forty years. It's habit."

We're sitting on Josh's back patio. It's partially covered, with a hanging swing on one side and a picnic table on the other and looks out over a large meadow where cattle are grazing.

"Do you get a lot of deer back here?" I ask.

He nods and swallows. "Usually in the evening and very early mornings. A moose walked through last week."

"That was cool," Seth murmurs, and Josh looks up in surprise.

Does Seth never talk to him?

"Yeah, it was," Josh agrees softly.

"Do you fish?" Seth asks me as he takes a big bite out of a chicken breast, sending golden pieces of fried batter down the front of his shirt. His dark hair is a bit too long and falls over one eye. I grin at him. He's adorable.

"No. I hate fishing."

"How can you hate to fish?!" Seth exclaims, as if I'd just admitted to hating ice cream.

"It's dirty." I wrinkle my nose and Josh bursts out laughing.

"Everything here is dirty, sweetheart." Josh shakes his head and nudges me lightly with his elbow.

He's such a flirt!

"But you live in Montana!" Seth exclaims, examining me as if I were a science project, his chicken momentarily forgotten.

"I live in town, Seth. Always have. My dad loves to fish. I just never really got into it." I shrug and take a bite of delicious homemade potato salad.

"But you like horses, right?" He shovels a heaping forkful of potato salad into his mouth.

"I've never ridden one." I chuckle and shake my head as I watch him eat. "Are they starving you here, Seth? The way you're eating, you'd think you haven't seen food in days."

Seth just blinks at me. He slowly smiles, but I cut him off before he can voice the idea I can see forming in that sharp brain of his.

"I'm not getting on a horse."

"Why not?" Josh asks with a broad smile.

"Well…" I look back and forth between the two guys and then sigh when I can't come up with a good reason not to. "I'm not dressed for riding."

Josh's gaze falls to my red sundress before his brown eyes find mine again. "Wear jeans tomorrow."

"I'm not here to learn how to ride a horse, I'm here to teach Seth."

"No reason that you can't do both," Josh replies with a grin, and winks at me, his dimple creasing his cheek, waking those butterflies in my stomach.

"Am I keeping you from work?" I change the subject and pop a piece of watermelon in my mouth, doing my best not to squirm in my chair.

"I have to go paint the fence," Seth mutters, and swigs down the last of his Coke, making me laugh.

"What?" he asks.

"When I drove up to the house and saw the white fence, I thought to myself, 'I don't envy the person who has to paint this every couple of years.' "

"It was either paint the fence or shovel the horse shit," Seth replies matter-of-factly.

"Mouth!" Josh scowls, pinning Seth with a look, and Seth rolls his eyes.

"Horse crap."

"I think I'd take the fence too," I agree, but Seth just shrugs his thin shoulders and frowns. "You look so much like your dad." I shake my head and reach for another piece of watermelon before I realize that both Seth and Josh have gone still.

"I do not," Seth whispers.

"Well, you look just like your uncle Josh, and Josh and Zack are twins, so…" I tilt my head to one side and watch Seth's face tighten.

"I'm nothing like my dad," he insists.

"Okay, I'm sorry."

Seth pins me with a scowl, then grabs his trash and lets himself into the house to dump it, stalks through the house, and slams the front door behind him.

"I'm sorry," I whisper again.

"It's okay. He's pissed at my brother. Won't talk about it, just won't have anything at all to do with him." Josh purses his lips and sighs, still watching the path Seth took through the house. My eyes are glued to his lips and I'm mortified to realize that I want him to kiss me.

And not just a sweet thank-you-for-teaching-my-nephew kiss, but a long, slow kiss that lasts forever and makes me forget how to breathe. I want to sink my fingers into his thick, dark hair and feel his large, callused hands glide down my back as he pulls me against him.

I want him to touch me.

Josh begins to pack up the remains of our lunch and I take a deep breath and join him.

"When he smiled at you earlier? That's the first

time I've seen him smile since he's been here."

"Josh, I'm so sorry. He's a great kid, and he's really smart. I think we'll have him back on track with his grades without a problem."

"Thank you." Josh replaces the lid on the fruit and throws it in the cooler. "You know, Kyle didn't tell me who he was sending out here. I was surprised when I saw it was you."

"Why?"

"I don't know, but I'm glad you're here. I wasn't kidding before—you look fantastic."

I blush and concentrate on rewrapping the chicken and placing it in the cooler.

"I'm not a hermit, Josh. Like I said before, you've seen me around."

"In passing. Not like this. I like it."

I stand up and cross my arms over my chest, then frown when he stands too and is more than a foot taller than me.

I've always been so damn short.

"Are you flirting with me?" I ask.

"Maybe." He pushes the lid down on the ice chest, then moves around the table to stand right next to me, and I have to tilt my head way back to see his eyes. "You always were a little thing."

"Little?! Oh my God." I giggle and throw a hand over my mouth. "I'm just short. Hell, in high school I was f—"

"If you say fat, I will take you over my knee, Carolina. You were not fat then, you're not fat now, and next to me, you are tiny." He sets his mouth in a disapproving line and pulls on a lock of my hair. "Your pretty blond hair is soft."

"Don't f-flirt with me," I stutter halfheartedly. Instead of moving away, I sway toward him, my heart racing.

"Why not?" He grins and continues to gently pull my hair between his thumb and forefinger, watching the strands as they fall out of his grasp.

"Because I'm your employee for the summer, and I like my job. It's not like there are dozens of middle schools here in town that I can work at if I get fired." I step away, pulling myself together, doing my best to remind myself of the blonde I saw leaving his house this morning and how I do not want to be another notch in Josh King's bedpost. I open his sliding screen door and gather my tote bag and purse and turn to find him standing right behind me again. "I have to go."

He sighs, props his hands on his hips, and looks as if he wants to say more, so I turn on my heel and walk briskly to the door.

"I'll walk you out," he mutters, and walks quickly to keep up with me. He holds his front door open for me, and I feel his hand on my lower back as he guides me to my little blue car.

He opens the door for me and settles my bags into the passenger seat.

"You're very chivalrous," I inform him dryly.

As I move to sit in the driver's seat, he runs his hand down my bare arm, very much as he did with Blondie this morning, and smiles.

"Thanks for doing this, Cara. Don't forget to wear jeans tomorrow." With that he winks and shuts my door, stepping back to watch me drive away.

Looks like I'll be wearing shorts tomorrow.